CALLIE FOR PRESIDENT

by ROBIN WASSERMAN

candy
apple

SCHOLASTIC INC.

New York Toronto London Auckland Sydney
Mexico City New Delhi Hong Kong Buenos Aires

For Alexis Offen, who will always have my vote

No part of this publication may be
reproduced, stored in a retrieval system,
or transmitted in any form or by any means,
electronic, mechanical, photocopying, recording,
or otherwise, without written permission of the publisher.
For information regarding permission, write to Scholastic Inc.,
Attention: Permissions Department,
557 Broadway, New York, NY 10012.

ISBN-13: 978-0-545-02220-0
ISBN-10: 0-545-02220-7

Copyright © 2008 by Robin Wasserman

12 11 10 9 8 7 6 5 4 3   8 9 10 11 12 13/0
40
Printed in the U.S.A.
First printing, May 2008

☆ CHAPTER ONE ☆

I do not hate school.

I mean it.

I do not hate the stench that oozes out of the cafeteria on meat loaf Mondays. Even if it does make everything in my locker smell like something that died on the side of the highway.

I do not hate the girls' bathroom on the second floor, where two of the toilets are always broken and the third is almost always surrounded by a suspicious-looking puddle.

I do not hate the stink bombs that go off in the middle stairwell every afternoon. I do not hate Jordan Pollet, the eighth grader with bad skin and worse breath, whose favorite hobby is lobbing spitballs at me from the back of our school bus. I do not hate my math teacher's monotone; the

1

sticky, crumb-spattered gunk covering every seat in the cafeteria; or even the marching band's perky grins when they parade through my homeroom every Friday morning and interrupt my nap.

Yes, Susan B. Anthony Middle School has room for improvement. *Plenty* of room. But I don't hate it.

"Don't say hate," my mom always tells me. "Words matter. Don't use that one unless you really mean it."

So I use other words instead. Words that I mean. Words like *detest. Despise. Loathe. Abhor.* (That one's my favorite.) And okay, I admit it, I use these words a lot — but there's a lot out there not to hate. A lot to detest, despise, loathe, and seriously, seriously abhor. My top three?

1. *Gym class*
2. *Brianna Blake*
3. *Wednesdays*

Gym class, because it's inhuman. Brianna Blake, because *she's* inhuman.

And Wednesdays most of all — because that's when I'm stuck with them both. At the same time.

"I'd make her do quadratic equations twenty-four seven," my best friend Maxine Samuels suggested. *Her* was the girls' gym teacher, Ms. Soderberg. (I don't hate her, either — though sometimes it's tempting.) Max and I were stranded deep in left field, brainstorming creative ways to torture our enemies. And since it was Ms. Soderberg's fault that we were shivering in the middle of a muddy field, with only our mucus-green Susan B. Anthony T-shirts and mandatory orange shorts to protect us from the cold, she was enemy number one.

It beat paying attention to the game.

We were two months into seventh grade — plenty of time to perfect the art of the outfield. The secret was choosing the perfect spot. It had to be far enough from home plate that we could safely avoid the ball for yet another week. If I had my way, that would mean the parking lot. Or better yet, the fro-yo shop down the street, where there were sixteen flavors and zero chance of getting hit in the head with a softball. But Ms. Soderberg had eagle eyes — if we backed *too* far away from home plate, she would catch on. Then, to encourage us to "Dig deep and play hard!" she would come up with something truly heinous, like make me play shortstop and send Max to second base.

Been there, done that. And all I can say is: never again.

So every Wednesday, we found ourselves a Goldilocks spot on the softball field — not too far, not too near, but just right. We fixed our eyes on the pitcher's mound and muttered to each other without moving our mouths. Every once in a while, we let out a cheer. Sometimes, it was even for our own team.

Some teachers feel like they have to treat all their students the same, no matter what. They say things like "There are no dumb questions," and "Every student deserves a chance to learn."

Ms. Soderberg was not one of those teachers.

By the second week of September last year, she discovered that Max and I couldn't run very fast.

We also couldn't throw very hard.

We couldn't catch, period.

So by the third week of September, she discovered that she had no use for us. By the fourth week of September, she discovered that she couldn't stand us. By October, she discovered that we felt exactly the same way.

After that, it was war.

True, Ms. Soderberg had most of the weapons on her side. She was the one who could make us run laps if we weren't paying attention, or give us detention when we forgot our gym uniforms. She could force us to do push-ups or ask us to (*try*) to serve a volleyball while the rest of the class pointed and laughed.

Which they did.

All we could do was stand in the outfield and glare — and plot elaborate ways to get back at her. You know, in case we ever found a magical portal into a fantasy world where kids made the rules and teachers just had to deal.

I shook my head at Max. "Quadratic equations? Way too easy. I say, force her to 'volunteer' for a dunk tank in the middle of December, in only her bathing suit —"

We both shivered at the thought of Ms. Soderberg in a bathing suit.

"— then let Jackson Cummings pelt tennis balls at the bull's-eye all day long," I finished. Jackson Cummings was the starting pitcher for the JV baseball team, and he had dead aim. I should know. After all, at last year's winter carnival, I was the one who had to "volunteer" for the dunk tank.

It was Ms. Soderberg's idea.

"Is it time to go in yet?" I asked, rubbing my bare arms. All the little hairs along them were standing at attention, and I was pretty sure I'd just felt a raindrop splash on my head. I looked up to see a flock of birds flying past. At least I hoped it was a raindrop. "It's *got* to be time to go in."

"One more out," Max reported.

My eyes widened. "Are you actually *paying attention*?"

Max blushed and ran a hand through her straw-straight black hair. "You're not the one who had to run ten laps last week for 'inattention in the outfield.'" She shuddered. "By lap five, I was ready to puke."

"Speaking of puking . . ." I pointed toward home plate.

Brianna Blake had stepped up to bat.

Brianna was wearing the same putrid gym uniform as the rest of us, but somehow on her, it looked runway-ready. Despite the misty wind, her blond hair was just as smooth, shiny, and frizz-free as ever. As she gripped the bat, her glossed lips spread in a wide smile, revealing two perfect rows of shiny white teeth that would never need braces. Unlike me, Brianna Blake loved gym.

Almost as much as she loved Brianna Blake.

Of course, she wasn't the only one. *Everyone* loved Brianna Blake. At Susan B. Anthony Middle School, it was pretty much a crime not to. Which made Max and me outlaws — just the way we liked it.

"Back it up!" our pitcher shouted, waving the outfielders farther out. "Wayyyyy back!"

Fine with me. "Way back" was exactly where I wanted to be. I went as far back as I could, to the point where the grass met the cement track circling the field.

The first ball went flying. Brianna didn't swing.

"Ball one!" Ms. Soderberg boomed. "Good eye, Brianna!"

A second pitch whistled across the plate. Still no swing.

"Just waiting for the perfect pitch," Brianna sang out.

"Just waiting for my brain transplant," Max murmured, making her voice nearly as high and sugar-sweet as Brianna's.

So I blame Max for what happened next.

Because I was laughing too hard to see the third pitch. I didn't see it sail right across the middle of home plate. I didn't see Brianna *finally* decide to take a swing. I just heard the crack of the bat. And by that time, it was too late.

The ball soared up, up, up ... but not quite away.

Instead, the ball hurtled way out into left field. So far out that there was only one person standing beneath it, one person too slow or too dumb to get out of the way. And that person was not Max. She'd darted into right field as soon as the ball made contact with the bat. I was the one who froze, my glove stretched to the sky, thinking:

This is all Brianna Blake's fault.

Thinking: *I'm going to miss the ball, and my team's going to lose, and everyone's going to want to kill me.*

Thinking: *Maybe this time . . .*

Maybe, just maybe . . .

Maybe I'll be the hero. Maybe I'll be the winner. Maybe I'll actually catch —

The ball thudded off the corner of my glove and bounced to the ground. I scooped it up just as Brianna slid into home for the winning run.

I guess I should have known. There was only room for one winner at Susan B. Anthony Middle School.

And it wasn't me.

"Woo-hoo!" Jacob Fisher hooted as I stepped out of the locker room. "Here she comes, our very own Johnny Damon!"

I glared at Max, who always managed to make it out of the locker room before me. Max made it *everywhere* before me. Probably because she defined "on time" as "ten minutes early," while I defined it as "considering the fact that I forgot/

overslept/lost track of time/couldn't find my left shoe, you should be happy I showed up at all."

"You just had to tell him, didn't you?" I said.

Jacob Fisher, aka Fish, aka my best friend ever since I conked him on the head with a dump truck in Mrs. Holland's preschool day care, was sprawled out on a bench in the gym lobby. His gym class met the same period ours did. That was the only good thing about Wednesdays — we always met up afterward to complain, before heading to our next class. At least, we usually complained.

Sometimes, we mocked.

"Max didn't have to tell me," Fish teased. "It's all over school. Word is, you're the next Derek Jeter."

I narrowed my eyes. "I'll give you ten bucks if you can tell me which team Derek Jeter *or* Johnny Damon plays for."

"They're baseball players, right?"

"Of course they're baseball players!" Max cried, exasperated. When it comes to Fish, she's almost always exasperated. Max is my best friend — and so's Fish. But that doesn't exactly mean they're best friends with each other.

Back in the old days, when homework meant coloring in a picture of George Washington's cherry tree and a busy day at school meant one nap time instead of two, Fish used to hate Max. Mostly because I told him to. I figured she was an obnoxious know-it-all-suck-up-teacher's-pet. Mostly because she was. (Well, all except the teacher's-pet part. Teachers love it when you're a know-it-all . . . until you know more than they do. Even at age eight, Max always did.)

Then came third grade. Max and I sat next to each other in the back row of Ms. Caldwell's class-room. Every day, while Ms. Caldwell droned on, Max and I would whisper-fight. About anything. About *everything*: whether erasable pens really worked. Why chocolate ice cream was superior to vanilla. Which Powerpuff Girl was most annoying. What the right way was to eat an Oreo.

The day of the Oreo fight was the day we forgot to whisper. "Lick the cream!" I shouted, right in the middle of Ms. Caldwell's lecture on the life cycle of a caterpillar. Before Max could shout back, "Dunk and chomp!" (again), we both got sent into the hallway to "think about our outburst." Instead, we thought about creative ways to get back at Ms. Caldwell. The rest is history.

Fish took a little while to get used to the idea that our twosome was going to be a threesome. A *very* little while. Like, about an hour. He just said that if I was cool with Max, he was, too. And the three of us have been hanging out ever since. Max is still a know-it-all, Fish is even flakier than I am, and both of them get grossed out watching me eat an Oreo, but somehow, the three of us just work. Always have — always will.

"What do you mean, 'are they baseball players?'" I asked Fish now, rolling my eyes. "What did you think they were?"

Fish shrugged. "Dunno. I heard my brothers yelling their names at the TV last night. Figured I'd take a shot."

Max rolled her eyes at me. "Your best friend is even more clueless about sports than you are."

Fish waved his sketch pad at Max. "And *your* best friend knows I have better things to do than waste my time with a bunch of Neanderthals throwing projectiles at each other. I have my *Art*."

Fish always says it that way, so that you can almost hear the capital *A*. He puts on a fake British accent, so it sounds more like "*Ahhhrt*." That's so everyone knows he's joking, and that art isn't really that important to him.

But here's the thing: It is.

Art is everything to him.

Everything except for me and Max, of course. Even an *ahhhrtist* has to have his priorities straight.

I ran my fingers through my hair. Or at least, what was left of it. At the beginning of the summer, my hair had been as long as my waist. So one day, in the middle of a heat wave, I decided to give myself a haircut.

Let's just say that's harder than it looks.

"Since we all agree that gym class is a form of medieval torture, not to mention a complete waste of time," I said, "can we just forget about my, uh . . ."

"Catastrophically klutzy, thoroughly humiliating, game-blowing miss?" Fish suggested.

"Yeah, that." I thwapped him lightly on the head with my notebook. "Let's just go, okay? We're going to be late for social studies."

"Late?" Fish asked. "The bell hasn't even rung yet."

"She just wants more face time with Mr. Hamilton," Max teased.

I could feel my cheeks heating up. *What can I use to cover my face?* I thought frantically. There had to be something. And quick, before they realized I was blushing.

Too late.

"Busted!" Max cried, sputtering with laughter.

Fish shook his head in disgust. "What is it with all you girls and Mr. Hamilton?" he asked. "He's not that —"

"Handsome?" Max supplied. "Brilliant? Funny? Cool?" She patted Fish on the shoulder. "News flash, Fish: He totally is. Just because you wish *you* were that cool . . ."

"Do not!" Fish protested, jerking away. "Like I'd want all those girls drooling all over me."

"I am *not* drooling," I said indignantly.

"I'm sorry, I didn't mean to overhear," a high, sweet voice piped up from behind me. "But do you need a tissue?"

Max went pale. Fish snorted, trying to hold back a laugh. I froze.

It wasn't real, I told myself. It was just a nightmare. Or a hallucination. That voice — that sickening, nauseating, all-too-familiar voice — was only in my head. It had to be. Because otherwise, it would mean that Brianna Blake was standing behind me, offering me a tissue to mop up my drool. If I turned around, if I actually *saw* her, it would be real. But if I could just keep my back to her until she got bored and walked away, I could

13

pretend that the whole thing had never happened. That would be the smart thing to do. Unfortunately, it wouldn't be the *Callie* thing to do.

I turned around.

"No thanks," I said to Brianna, in a tight voice. I wasn't nervous. Just because Brianna Blake was the most popular girl in school, just because she had never before bothered to speak to someone like *me*, there was no reason to be nervous. Brianna Blake didn't impress me. And she definitely didn't *scare* me. "I'm fine. Thanks."

I gave her a smile so tiny you would have needed a microscope to prove it was there. Then I waited for her to leave. Obviously she'd made some kind of colossal mistake coming over to talk to me. It was kind of dark in the lobby — maybe from a distance, she'd thought I was someone else. Now that we were face-to-face, she would surely escape as quickly as she could.

Except she didn't.

"How are you doing, Callie?" she asked sweetly. She had a hint of a southern accent. It didn't make any sense, because she was born right here in New Jersey, just like the rest of us. I knew for a fact that the only time she'd ever even *been* to the south was on a family trip to Disney World in the third grade. Even so, her mouth drawled molasses with

14

every word. "It's been such a long time since we chatted."

Brianna Blake was the only seventh grader in the world who "chatted."

"I'm fine," I said. This time, I gave her a nano-smile.

"And how about you, Michelle?" she asked.

There was a long pause. Suddenly, Fish snickered, and poked Max in the shoulder. "I think that's you," he whispered loudly.

"It's *Max*," Max corrected her. "As in Maxine. We've known each other since kindergarten."

Brianna Blake giggled. It sounded like two glasses clinking together. "Of course, how silly of me. Max. What a *cute* nickname."

There was something about the way she said "cute." You could tell she meant "babyish."

"And Jacob!" Brianna flung her hands out to her sides. "I've been looking *everywhere* for you!"

Fish looked behind him, like he couldn't believe she actually meant *him*. "Uh, most people call me Fish, but —"

"Why?" Brianna wrinkled her nose. "Jacob's such a great name. Strong and sensitive at the same time, you know? So much nicer than" — she wrinkled her nose even more, as if she was breathing in the stench of rotten trout — "*Fish*."

15

I tried to catch Fish's eye. We've known each other for so long that sometimes we don't have to talk. I can just lock eyes with him and think, *Can you believe her?* And he totally gets it, every time.

Except this time, Fish wasn't even looking in my direction. He was looking at Brianna. And he was grinning. "Yeah, maybe," he admitted. "Jacob's cool, too."

"Fish, we should probably get going," I said, giving him another Look. This one said: *I'm throwing you a life preserver. Grab it.*

This time, he looked back — and shrugged.

"So . . . what's going on, Brianna?" he asked her. Like they were friends or something.

Brianna gave us her whitest, brightest, toothpaste-commercial grin. "You guys know what day it is today, right?"

Max and I glanced at each other. "Uh, Wednesday?" Max finally guessed.

Brianna threw her head back and laughed. Her shoulders shook, her blond hair bobbed up and down, and, like magic, her two best friends popped up beside her, laughing even harder. It didn't matter that they hadn't heard the joke. Or that there was no joke. If Brianna thought something was funny, they did, too.

"Today is the start of campaign season!" Brianna cried.

Max stared blankly back at her. Fish leaned forward on the metal bench and began doodling something on one of his sneakers. But Brianna seemed to be waiting for something.

"Campaign for what?" Max finally asked.

Brianna's two friends, Britney and Ashton, looked at us like we were nuts. "For class council *president?*" Britney asked. Everything that came out of her mouth always sounded like a question. "Brianna's totally going to win?"

"Like she does every year!" Ashton gushed, twirling a finger through her long, wavy hair. At the beginning of the year she'd tried to dye it blond to match Brianna's, but something must have gone wrong. It had turned a froggy shade of green instead. "I don't even know why we bother to *have* an election."

I didn't, either. Brianna Blake had been our class council president since fourth grade, when we first started *having* class council presidents. She always won 100 percent of the votes. Maybe because no one ever bothered to run against her.

That didn't stop her from campaigning. Every year, for two weeks, the halls would be wallpapered with neon posters urging us to VOTE FOR BLAKE, SHE'S NO FAKE! and SIMON SAYS, BLAKE FOR PRES!

She used the same lame slogans every year. How inspiring.

"Okay, well, good luck," Fish told her, and he sounded like he really meant it. He probably did. That's the thing about Fish. He's nice to everyone.

"She doesn't need luck?" Britney sort-of-asked. "She's Brianna Blake?"

Brianna covered her cheeks with her palms, like she was blushing with modesty. But I could see through her fingers, and her cheeks were just as pale and perfect as always. "It's not me," she protested. "I've got a great campaign team. And, um —" She cleared her throat. Even a normally gross noise like that came out sounding ladylike when Brianna made it. "That's why I'm here, Jacob. Everyone knows you're the best artist in school."

Now it was Fish's turn to fake-blush, but he didn't bother. It's not that he's stuck-up or anything, he just knows how good he is. Everyone does. Even Brianna, it turned out. And that's when I suddenly realized what she wanted from Fish.

"And you know, running a campaign means making lots of posters and everything, so I thought, maybe . . ." It wasn't like Brianna to stammer and babble. "Do you want to be on my campaign?"

18

Max gasped.

Fish looked up from his doodling. He narrowed his eyes, like he was trying to figure out whether she was teasing him.

"Really," Brianna went on, "you could make some amazing posters." She turned to Britney and Ashton. "Don't you think?"

They bobbed their heads up and down. Of course, they would have done that no matter what Brianna asked them.

You should go dunk your heads in the toilet, don't you think?

And they would nod, *Yes, yes, of course, yes.*

"So will you?" Brianna asked. She opened her bright blue eyes wide, like an anime character, and twisted her mouth into a dainty pout.

I waited for Fish to tell her no way, no how, no chance would he ever, *ever* help her wiggle her way into power for yet another year. Fish would say it nicely, because that was just the kind of guy he was. But he would still say it: *No.* That wasn't a word Brianna Blake heard very often. I couldn't wait.

Fish tapped his pen against the top of his sneaker, which used to be white before he covered it with his green-and-blue ballpoint doodles.

This was it, finally. Brianna Blake's very first no.

"Yeah," Fish said, grinning. "Okay. Why not?"

☆ CHAPTER TWO ☆

"Are you crazy?" I whispered, leaning across the aisle toward Fish's desk.

He stared straight ahead. But he couldn't fool me. Fish had never in his life paid attention in social studies class, and I was pretty sure he wasn't starting any time soon.

"Fish!" I hissed. "*Fish!* How can you agree to work on Brianna's campaign?"

"Shhh!" Fish finally turned toward me, crossed his eyes, stuck out his tongue, then whipped his head back around to the front of the class. I sighed. Fish could never take anything seriously. Not even something like *this*.

Max, who sat behind me, tapped me on the shoulder. She tipped her glittery orange pen toward Mr. Hamilton, who was trying — and failing — to explain to us why anyone would ever want to run for class office. Mr. Hamilton was the faculty sponsor for the seventh grade class council, which meant he had to pretend he cared. The rest of us didn't.

"Definitely a new shirt," Max whispered. "I give it a six." I shook my head, and held up four fingers, biting down on the corners of my lips so I wouldn't laugh.

Here's the thing about Mr. Hamilton. He may be a teacher, and he may be kind of old (though not as old as, like, my dad) but he doesn't act like it. He wears green Converse sneakers that are almost as beat-up as my pink ones — but his aren't duct-taped together. His hair is always sticking straight up, and rumor is, he plays bass guitar in a band on the weekends.

Basically, he's cool.

And I don't mean cool like Brianna Blake and her posse. Because they're not cool, they're popular. Trust me, there's a difference.

He's cool like some indie punk rocker who's too cool to be on the radio, cool like he should be working in a coffee shop in New York City and writing poetry on the side — way too cool for Susan B. Anthony Middle School. But the weird thing is, he acts like he wants to be here. He acts like he actually likes teaching and seventh graders and social studies. He gets all excited about whatever he's teaching us, and no matter how boring we think it's going to be, he gets us excited, too.

Which may be the coolest thing of all.

Mr. Hamilton wears a different T-shirt every day, usually with the name of some band no one's ever heard of. Some of them are sort of cool, some of them are très cool, and some of them are ultra cool. (That day's shirt was gray with black lettering across the front reading: SOUL ASYLUM, whatever that meant.) Max and I developed a rating system. It kept us awake during the very rare moments when Mr. Hamilton was being kind of boring.

Like now.

"And of course, the class council president will be in charge of planning the year's big fund-raising event, which is traditionally a winter carnival," Mr. Hamilton droned. You got the feeling that even *he* was bored. "And at the end of the year, the president will work with the rest of the council to decide how the money will be spent."

Max snorted. I knew what she was thinking. Mr. Hamilton made it sound like some big mystery. But we all knew how the money would be spent. Just like every other year, Brianna Blake would run, Brianna Blake would win, then Brianna Blake and her buddies would raise money with a winter carnival and spend it all on a big spring dance. A spring dance that nobody but Brianna Blake and her buddies wanted to go to. Who wants to spend a Saturday night standing around the gym, drinking raspberry punch and breathing in the stench of sweat socks?

I'll tell you who: Brianna Blake.

She was sitting front and center, same as she does in every class, staring up at Mr. Hamilton like every word out of his mouth was the most amazing sound she'd ever heard. Her seat gave her a much better view of Mr. Hamilton's T-shirt collection, but my seat way in the back gave me the chance to ball up tiny pieces of paper and flick them at Fish's head, trying to force him to turn around. It didn't work.

"And now, drumroll please . . . I'll open up the nominations for class council president!" Mr. Hamilton announced dramatically. Just when you thought Mr. Hamilton was different from all the rest of the teachers, he'd say something kind of cheesy to remind you that he belonged here after all. But I forgave him. Even cool people have to be uncool once in a while; it makes them even cooler. "Who would like to —"

"I nominate Brianna Blake?" Britney shouted,

jumping out of her seat and waving her hand in the air.

Brianna smiled and looked down at her desk, like she was embarrassed. But I knew it was just an act.

Mr. Hamilton nodded. "Okay, does anyone second the —"

"I second the nomination!" Ashton shrieked. She flashed Brianna a grin and a thumbs-up. Brianna ignored her. She fixed her laser stare on Mr. Hamilton instead and gave him her most dazzling smile.

"I'd be honored to be a candidate," she said sweetly, smoothing down her blond hair. Not that it ever needed smoothing. "It's such a privilege to be able to serve my school . . . I mean, *if* I win, of course."

Of course.

Mr. Hamilton didn't smile back.

I decided to up that day's T-shirt rating to a ten. Extra points for good behavior.

"Okay, so we have Brianna running," he said. "Anyone else?"

Silence.

Everyone knew that Brianna Blake wanted to be class council president, and everyone knew that what Brianna Blake wanted, Brianna Blake got.

Mr. Hamilton cleared his throat. "I'm sure *some-one* wants to run. An election is a great way to engage your civic consciousness — and we can't have a real campaign with only one candidate, now can we?"

"See?" I whispered to Fish. "It's not even a real campaign, so I don't know why you have to work on it."

Fish twisted around. "Maybe I *want* to," he whispered back.

"You're going to have to suck up to her, like all the rest of them," Max muttered.

Fish wiggled his eyebrows and gave us an evil grin. "What if I make *her* suck up to me instead? Ever think of that?"

I rolled my eyes. Fish didn't get it. Once he got dragged into Brianna Blake's evil vortex of shallowness, there'd be no escape. She was like a black hole of blond. "Why don't you just tell her you changed your —"

"Callie?" Mr. Hamilton said, waving at me. "I hate to interrupt your very important conversation, but we're kind of in the middle of something up here."

I could feel my face turning tomato red. "Oh, uh, sorry, Mr. Hamilton. I, uh . . . sorry."

He raised his eyebrows. "Care to share your thoughts with the rest of the class?"

"I . . . um . . ." I took a deep breath. "I don't have any thoughts right now, Mr. Hamilton."

The whole class started laughing, even Max and Fish.

"How about you, Max?" Mr. Hamilton asked. Max's giggles morphed into a cough. "You've *always* got something to say."

"Oh, uh, we were, uh, just —"

"Maybe you were about to express your civic duty by throwing your hat into the ring?" he asked.

"What?" Max wrinkled her forehead.

Mr. Hamilton gave her an encouraging smile. "The topic of today's discussion is the race for class council president," he reminded her. "And it occurs to me that, given your interest in history and politics, perhaps you'd like to —"

"I nominate Callie!" Max yelped.

I almost jumped out of my seat. *"What?"* I whirled around to glare at her. She shrugged, and mouthed *sorry.* But that wasn't going to cut it.

"Callie Singer?" I heard someone mutter. It sounded like Britney. "You've got to be kidding?"

Fish's hand shot into the air. "I second the nomination!" he shouted, loud and clear.

26

For the second time that day, I closed my eyes and wished that I was in the middle of a dream.

For the second time that day, my wish didn't come true. And when I opened my eyes, Mr. Hamilton's Soul Asylum T-shirt was staring me in the face.

"Congratulations, Callie," he said as I glared at Fish and Max, wishing for laser-powered eyes that could burn holes right through my former best friends' foreheads. "Looks like you're running for president."

"How *could* you?" I cried as soon as we escaped from the classroom.

"Problem, Madame President?" Fish asked innocently.

"What were you thinking?" I shook Max by the shoulders. "Are you trying to torture me?"

Max wriggled out of my grasp. "You're the one who's always whining about how Brianna Blake wins everything," she pointed out, pushing her glasses up on her nose. "Now's your chance to beat her."

"Beat her?" I asked, my eyes widening. "*Beat her?* Didn't you hear everyone in there" — I winced — "laughing at me? They know I can't beat Brianna. Nobody can. But you two, my supposed best

27

friends . . ." It's hard to talk when your heart is thumping in your chest, and your brain is stuffed full of one thought repeated a million times: *What am I going to do now? What am I going to do now? WhatamIgoingtodonow . . . ?*

So whatever came out of me next — half squeak, half growl — wasn't quite in English. But it got the point across. I turned my back on the two of them and started speed-walking to the cafeteria. I needed a serious sugar rush to wash the last hour out of my system.

But it's harder to get rid of best friends than bad memories. They followed me.

"I'm sorry," Max said, tugging at my shoulder. "I just blurted it out before I knew what I was saying. I didn't mean to."

"Well, *I* did," Fish said indignantly. "You'd make a great president, Callie. And you're always saying that someone should run against Brianna. Why not you?"

"You *would* be good," Max said hesitantly. "And you have plenty of opinions about how to run things."

"Yeah, you're always bossing *us* around," Fish pointed out.

Max gave him a light shove. "We're supposed to

be apologizing," she reminded him in a stage whisper. "Save the insults for *after* she forgives us."

I rolled my eyes. "You know *she's* standing right here, right? And you're definitely not forgiven yet."

I stopped at my locker to ditch my books before lunch. Max leaned back against the metal doors, her eyes glowing. "Think about the possibilities," she said. "You're always complaining how the class council never does anything for people like us, right?"

"The class council doesn't know that people like us exist," I grumbled.

"And you love bossing people around," Fish added — and once was more than enough.

I gave him a light shove. "I love bossing *you* around."

"How many times a day do you start a sentence with 'If I were in charge around here'?" Max asked.

"Once a week," I said. "Maybe."

Fish snorted. "Try ten times a day. *At least.*"

"This could be our chance — I mean, your chance," Max continued, "to tell the school what you *really* think. And make them realize that just because Brianna's blond and beautiful —"

"Not *that* beautiful," I interrupted.

"Just because people *think* she's blond and beautiful —"

"Well, she really *is* blond," Fish pointed out. "I don't think you can call that a matter of opinion."

Max slammed her palm flat against the locker. "It's not just about Brianna Blake!" she sputtered. "It's about taking a stand against all the lame stuff that this school throws at us every day. We could actually change the way things are done. We could actually —"

"Make a difference?" I guessed, only half teasing. Sure, it sounded cheesy and after-school special-y. But it also sounded kind of good. Max and Fish were right. I *did* have a lot to say. And there were plenty of things I would change about Susan B. Anthony Middle School if I got the chance.

But I suddenly realized that was a pretty big *if.*

"You guys, you're forgetting one big thing," I told them. "Even if I wanted to be president," I continued, "and I'm not saying I do, but even *if*, I'd still have to win. How am I supposed to do that?"

"Easy." Max beamed. "I'll be your campaign manager. With me on your side, we can't lose."

Oh, boy. "Um, Max, I know you're into this kind of thing," I began hesitantly, "and you always know about presidents and wars and prime ministers and stuff in other countries, but . . ." I didn't want to offend her. And after all, she was the only seventh grader I knew who read the *International Herald Tribune* every day, whatever that was. "Do you really think knowing about the gross national product of Zimbabwe is going to help us win a class council election in central New Jersey?"

Max folded her arms across the chest. Her Look was a Max Special: cocky, irritated, excited, and calm, all at the same time.

"I'm going to pretend I didn't hear that," she said. "How long have we been friends?"

"Four years," I replied.

"And have I ever *not* known enough about anything?" she asked.

"She's like a walking encyclopedia," Fish pointed out. "It's annoying."

To anyone else, that would be an insult, but Max smiled. "Thanks."

I banged my head back against my locker, defeated. "Okay, you got me."

"You're in?" Max asked excitedly.

"Only if you really promise to run my campaign for me. Like you said, with you guys on my side, how can I lose?"

"Uh, about that," Fish began, then stopped. He pulled out a pen and knelt down for some emergency sneaker-doodling. But I knew him too well: Fish

31

only does that when he's trying to get out of looking someone in the eye. So I crouched down next to him and snatched the pen out of his hand. Then I stared at him, silently daring him to look away. He didn't.

"About *what*?" I asked.

"About the whole 'you guys on my side' thing," Fish said. "You need to change that to 'guy.' Singular. Or, if you want to get technical, *girl*."

"What's that supposed to mean?"

Fish sighed. "Callie, you know I want you to win. I'm the one who seconded the nomination, remember?"

"But . . ."

"But I already told Brianna I'd help with her campaign."

"So? Just tell her you changed your mind."

"I gave her my word," Fish said. "I can't just take it back now."

"You're really going to work for the enemy?" Max asked like she couldn't believe it. I know I couldn't.

"It doesn't have to be a big deal," Fish said. "Uh . . . right?"

Max glared. "Of course it —"

"No," I said loudly, shooting Max a *Stop Talking* Look. "It doesn't. If you want to work on Brianna's campaign, that's" — *Traitorous? Ridiculous? Insane? Unbelievable? The opposite of what my oldest and best friend in the world is supposed to do?* — "okay with me," I told him.

"Promise?" Fish asked. "We're all good? This won't change anything?"

"Promise." I nodded firmly, trying to sound like I was sure. "It won't change a thing."

☆ CHAPTER THREE ☆

But the changes started that afternoon.

We all took the bus home together, like always. We crossed the street and walked the six blocks along Oliver Road to my house, like always. I opened the door and waved Max and Fish inside so we could catch the end of our favorite show, *This Can't Be My Life*, like always.

But then I remembered the election — and I stopped. Max stepped into the doorway, blocking Fish from stepping inside.

"Problem?" he asked.

I didn't say anything. Neither did Max.

Fish tapped his watch. "Clock's ticking. Do you want to miss the show?"

Max cleared her throat and took a breath, like

she was about to say something. But she didn't. Instead, she turned toward me. "Tell him."

I shook my head. No way. "You tell him."

"Anyone want to fill me in?" Fish asked impatiently.

Max stared at me, but when I didn't say anything, she sighed. "Fine. The thing is, Fish, that, uh, well —"

"Wait!" I yelped. "I'll tell him. I'm the one running for president."

"It was my idea," Max pointed out, rolling her eyes at me.

True. And it had seemed like a pretty terrible one at first, but once I thought about it, I had to admit . . . it wasn't. "Your idea, but my decision, right? That's what you said. I'm the candidate."

"And I'm the manager, so let me manage," she said. "I'll tell him."

"He's *my* best friend."

"Which is exactly why you shouldn't have to —"

"Will someone just tell me?" Fish sighed.

"You can't come in," I blurted.

Fish wrinkled his forehead, then dug his fingers into his ears like he was trying to clear out the wax.

"I must have heard you wrong, because I thought you said —"

"You can't come in," I repeated. I glanced at Max, and she nodded. "Max and I have to have our first campaign meeting, and, uh . . . you can't come."

"Okay, very funny," Fish said, fake-laughing. "Now let me in, or we're going to miss the show."

"I'm not kidding," I said. I wished I was. But Max and I had talked it over after lunch, and even though neither of us liked it, we both agreed. Fish was working for Brianna, the enemy. Which made him the enemy, too. I felt bad kicking him out — but then, I also felt bad that he was working for Brianna in the first place. And he didn't seem to care. That was his call.

This was mine.

"We have a lot of stuff to do," I said, telling myself there was nothing to feel guilty about.

"*Secret* stuff," Max added.

Fish's eyebrows jumped up, but he just shrugged. "It's cool. I told Brianna I'd show her some of my poster ideas this afternoon, anyway. So, I guess . . . see ya."

"Yeah," I muttered, trying not to picture Fish hanging out on *Brianna's* couch, watching *This Can't Be My Life* on *Brianna's* TV. Which was probably a big flat-screen with high def and surround sound. What if he liked it so much over there that he never wanted to come back?

I told myself I couldn't worry about that. Max and I had work to do.

We had an election to win.

"See ya," I said finally. And I shut the door in his face.

"We should definitely be allowed off campus for lunch," I said, reading off my brainstorming list of campaign ideas. "And they should put the junk food back in the cafeteria vending machines. All those energy bars and health chips taste like cardboard. And what about homeroom? It's a total joke. If we got rid of it, that would be ten more minutes of sleep every morning —"

"Callie, maybe we should —"

But I barely heard Max. I was on a roll. "And there has to be some other kind of fund-raiser to have, instead of the stupid winter carnival. Like a bake sale. No, that's lame. Or maybe a bowl-a-thon — ugh, even lamer." I flopped backward onto my bed, rolling over on the comforter. Fish, Max, and I had sewn it together from a bunch of our old T-shirts and pajamas. It was pretty faded, and a lit-tle too Powerpuff Girly for my taste (blame Max's former obsession), but it was definitely cooler than the scratchy pink-flowered nightmare my mom had bought to match the curtains. "Maybe we shouldn't have a fund-raiser at all," I suggested. "Let everyone keep their money. Who needs a big end-of-the-year class activity, anyway? I'd rather stay home."

"I think you're missing the point," Max said. She was hunched over my desk, flipping through a thick green book I'd never seen before. "Before we decide what you're going to say, we have to figure out how to make them listen."

"How are they supposed to listen if I don't have anything to say?" I asked. "Shouldn't we be coming up with some actual issues? You know, give people a reason to vote for me?"

"First rule of elections," Max announced. "It doesn't matter what you're selling — it only matters how you sell it."

That didn't sound quite right to me. "First rule, according to who?"

Max spun around on the chair to face me. "You've got to trust me on this," she said. "I've done a little research, and I think I know how we're going to win this thing."

I choked back a laugh. "A *little* research?" I said, nodding toward the giant stack of books she'd lugged home from the library. "Is this like the time you did a *little* research on chocolate chip cookies and ended up baking *sixteen* batches in search of the perfect recipe?"

She grabbed the stuffed octopus perched on the edge of my desk and threw it at me. I ducked. "I didn't hear you complaining when you were stuffing your face with cookie dough," she pointed out.

"Um, maybe that's because I was too busy gagging on all that hot pepper you decided to throw in. And let's not even talk about the cream-cheese batch." You know how people are always saying that everything tastes like chicken? Well, Max's "chocolate cream-cheese delights" tasted like chicken, too . . . chicken slathered with dog food and cooked in turpentine soup.

"Okay, so there were a few missteps along the way," Max admitted. "But did we or did we not come up with the perfect recipe?"

"Books aren't made out of sugar and chocolate," I pointed out. "And we don't have time to chew through a hundred of them before we find the perfect one."

"Already done," she said, patting the top of the stack and looking pretty proud of herself.

"You read *all* of those?" I asked, eyes wide. "Since this morning?"

"Well, 'read' is an exaggeration," Max admitted. "But I skimmed enough to get the point. And most of them weren't worth reading, anyway." She held up a thick, reddish book. "This one? I'm surprised the author didn't fall asleep in the middle of writing it." She tossed it aside and grabbed another one. "And this one is written for three-year-olds. The guy actually defines the word *incumbent*. As if anyone reading this book isn't going to know what that means."

I laughed weakly. "Um, yeah. As if."

Max knew me well enough to see that I didn't know what it meant. Lucky for her, she also knew me well enough not to mention it.

"And *this* book," she continued. "It's like someone had food poisoning and turned their throw-up into a book —"

"Gross!" I cried, waving my hands at her to stop. I couldn't take any more, not when my stomach was still churning with the memory of Max's cream-cheese delights. "Stop, please! I get it. All the books stink. We're right back where we started. Clueless."

"Not *all* the books." She handed me the one she'd been reading earlier, the green one with thick yellow type across the front. Almost every page was marked with a neon-green sticky note.

"So You Want to Win," I read, "by Gerald P. Pinchon, PhD. This one's good?"

"Not just good," Max corrected me. "*Great*. Listen to this." She flipped open to one of the pages she'd marked. "'Rule number seven: A frown is worth a hundred votes — for your opponent.'" She flipped to another page. "And how about this? 'Rule number thirteen: Think big, talk bigger.'" She closed the book and slapped her hand down on the cover. "It's all in here. Every detail, every angle. It's a master blueprint for the perfect campaign. *This* is how we're going to win."

I recognized that look in her eye. It was the look that my mom called "getting swept away by her excitement." It was the look that I called "time to hide under the bed until the crazy girl gets bored and moves on to something else." Don't get me wrong, it's not a bad thing to have a best friend who has to know everything about *everything*. (Especially on the night before a social studies test when she has nine million study flash cards and I still haven't finished reading the chapter yet. Not that that's happened . . . more than four or five times. This year.) But my mom was right. Sometimes Max got a little carried away. And I wasn't sure I wanted my campaign to go with her.

"Max, I hate to break it to you, but there's no way we're actually going to win," I reminded her.

Maybe I was reminding myself, too. *"Brianna's* going to win. You know that. We're only running against her to make a point."

Max shook her head. "You just proved how perfect this book is." She opened it again and began to read. "'There comes a point in every campaign where the candidate feels winning is hopeless. Caution: *This* is the danger zone. Nothing is more damaging to a campaign than doubt. And nothing is more advantageous than certainty. Do not fear loss. Do not expect defeat. Rule number fourteen: Control your own fate. Choose to win.'"

I had to admit, I liked the sound of that: *Choose to win.* And I wanted to.

I just wasn't sure how.

"So what did you do in school today, Calliope?"

I didn't answer.

My mother had known me for twelve years, seven months, and four days. Long enough to figure out that I don't answer to that name.

"Callie, your mother asked you a question," my father said.

I shoved another mouthful of bean curd in my mouth, trying not to gag. This year, my parents decided that they were vegans.

Which meant *we* were vegans.

Lucky for me, they never found the box of frozen pizza I kept stashed in the back of the freezer. Some of *us* couldn't survive without cheese.

"Calliope?" my mother prodded. "You must have done something today."

I dropped my fork onto the plate. It clanged. "My name is Callie," I reminded her. "*Not* Calliope."

"Not according to your birth certificate," my mom pointed out, just like she always does. We have this argument approximately eleven times a week. And I never win. "I know, because I'm the one who signed it. And let me tell you, it was a pretty memorable day —"

"Okay!" I cried, waving my napkin in surrender. "Enough! You win!"

My mom gave me a wicked grin. She just loves to gross me out with the "miraculous story of my birth." It's her favorite way to win an argument.

And it works every single time.

My mother's the one who came up with the name Calliope. As in, Calliope the ancient Greek muse of epic poetry, subject of my mother's first book, *Muse to My Ears: The Search for Lyrical Immortality in Ancient Greece.* Now, I ask you: Who names their one and only daughter *Calliope*?

Answer: the same people who name their one and only son *Hobbes*. That one was my father's

43

oh-so-brilliant idea. *He* wrote his first book on the philosopher Thomas Hobbes. According to Hobbes, life is "nasty, brutish, and short."

Guess what?

So's my brother.

"Oh, pretty please," Hobbes said sarcastically, poking me in the side. "Tell us all about the *amazing* stuff you did today, *Calliope*. We can't wait."

"Hobbes, let Calliope speak her mind," my mother said.

That's how it goes. Not "Hobbes, stop torturing your little sister." Or "Hobbes, stop twisting the heads off of Calliope's Barbie dolls." And *never* "Hobbes, stop being such a stuck-up jerk who thinks he's better than everyone else just because he's on the high school football team."

My parents are big believers in speaking your mind. Even if, as in Hobbes's case, your mind is empty. They're always telling us we need to be ourselves and "explore every avenue of intellectual opportunity." They know all about intellectual avenues, since they're professors at the local college. Hobbes only knows about cute girls and football stats, but they're okay with that, too. They say he's "embarking on his *bildungsroman*, the time-honored journey from youth to manhood."

Hobbes loves it when they say that. But only because it sounds a little like *dung.* He'd rather take a journey to the Superbowl.

As for me? I'm not on any kind of journey.

Sometimes, I think my mom wishes Fish was her kid, instead of me. He's an artist, just like the people she studies. My dad loves Max, mostly because she lets him drone on and on . . . and *on* about whatever seventeenth-century dead guy is the topic of his next paper. And, unlike the rest of us, she actually pays attention.

Then there was me. I wasn't an artist and I wasn't an intellectual. I wasn't even a football star. I wasn't anything. Until that night.

That night, I realized, I was a *candidate.*

"Actually, I did do something in school today," I said. "I'm running for class council president."

My brother almost spit a mouthful of soy milk–flavored mashed potatoes all over the table-cloth. *"You?"*

"Why not me?" I asked. "I could make a great president."

Hobbes snorted.

"What do you know?" I snapped.

"Since when are you into any of that rah-rah school spirit stuff? Aren't you always whining about how lame it is?"

"It's not lame to want to improve your school," I said indignantly. "I think I could help."

"Oh yeah?" Hobbes said. "How?"

"I . . . uh . . . well . . ." Max and I hadn't gotten quite that far with our campaign strategy. We'd decided exactly how I was supposed to deliver my message . . . we just hadn't decided what that message was going to be.

"That school would be lucky to have your help, Calliope," my mother said proudly. "And I think it's wonderful that you've discovered an interest in the democratic process. You know, our word *democracy* actually derives from the ancient Greek. Athens has long been considered the first functioning democratic society."

"And, of course, we must remember what Hobbes says," my father added. " 'For the prosperity of a people ruled by an aristocratical or democratical assembly cometh not from aristocracy, nor from democracy, but from the obedience and concord of the subjects.' Advice I don't necessarily suggest you heed, since I'm sure blind obedience is no more common among your peers than it was in his!" My parents burst into laughter.

Hobbes and I just looked at each other. My brother may be a repulsive toad, but sometimes I think he's the only other sane person in our house.

my parents r krzy, I IMed Fish that night, just like I did every night. It was part of my bedtime ritual: do homework, brush teeth, put on pajamas, IM Fish about my parents' latest weirdness. Sometimes it was my favorite part of the day. There was something about sitting there in the dark, watching the words scroll across the screen. It was like I was alone and not alone, all at the same time. Like I could say anything, and he would understand.

FishingPole: I know. just like u!
Bubbagump: lol. not.

When Fish and I were kids, we watched some long, boring movie about this restaurant called Bubba Gump Shrimp. Fish thought that was so funny, he called me Bubba Gump for weeks. Lucky for me, it didn't stick — I was pretty sure Gerald P. Pinchon would veto a slogan like "Bubba Gump for President."

But it worked okay for a screen name.

FishingPole: u and max do all ur secret campaign stuff?

47

Bubbagump: yes. it took 4EVER. u?

FishingPole: not so bad. went over 2 brianna's.
she liked my ideas. then her mom took us for pizza.
B likes anchovies, 2!

I stopped typing. So while I was home trying to choke down Styrofoam-flavored mashed potatoes, Fish was having pizza with *Brianna*?

And not just any pizza.

Anchovy pizza.

Our pizza.

We always said we were the only two people in the world who liked that topping. Who was Brianna Blake to share *my* pizza topping with *my* best friend?

And what was he doing calling her "B"? Not "Brianna Blake." Not "the spoiled, uptight, putridly perky girl who fooled me into working on her campaign." Just *B*.

Like they were friends, or something.

Bubbagump: im jealous!

Bubbagump: of the pizza, I mean

Fishingpole: bean curd again?

Bubbagump: u guessed it

Fishingpole: yuck

Bubbagump: so, tell me!

Fishingpole: tell u what?

Bubbagump: u spent all afternoon w/the queen of darkness, u must have some good stories . . .

Fishingpole: don't be mean. she's not that bad

Bubbagump: not that bad? ur kidding, right?

Fishingpole: she's ok. and kind of funny, there was this 1 time when

Bubbagump: uh-oh, phone call, gotta go

Fishingpole: ok. l8r g8r

I clicked the window shut and changed my away message to "dreaming of ice cream."

I didn't know why I had lied to Fish about the phone call. I didn't mean to — it just popped out. I couldn't stand hearing some disgusting story about how great and funny *B* was. *Not* because I was jealous. Fish could be friends with whoever he wanted.

Besides, he wasn't *friends* with Brianna Blake, I reminded myself. He was just helping her out. Because he was a nice guy.

Just like I was a nice girl. Not mean, like Fish said. I just told the truth. Fish *used* to like that about me.

Part of me wanted to sign on to IM again so that I could tell Fish I lied about the phone call. Or maybe I could just tell him it was a wrong number, and we could start all over. I would even let him tell me about how great Brianna was, if he wanted. I would be the perfect friend. I would be *nice*.

But instead, I just turned out my lights and crawled into bed.

It took me a long time to fall asleep.

☆ CHAPTER FOUR ☆

We only had two weeks until the election, and Max didn't want to waste any time. Which meant that less than forty-eight hours after agreeing to run, I was standing on a bench, surrounded by glitter-spackled VOTE FOR CALLIE! posters.

"I feel like an idiot," I muttered. Max grinned and gave me a thumbs-up.

"Just smile," she said. "This is so going to work. We're doing everything by the book."

We were about to officially kick off my campaign with a big after-school rally. Mr. Hamilton had given us a pass to leave school a few minutes early so that we could get set up. We stood in a corner of the empty parking lot, waiting for the bell to ring. Max had brought in a stack of Tupperware filled with brownies, cupcakes, Rice Krispie Treats, and three batches of her perfect-recipe chocolate chip cookies. She laid them all out in neat rows along a metal folding table, then set out two piles of napkins and plastic forks.

I tried to grab a cookie. Max smacked my hand away.

"Do you want to greet your voters with chocolate in your teeth?" she asked.

"I want to greet them with chocolate in my stomach," I grumbled, gazing at one of the double-fudge walnut brownies I wasn't allowed to touch. "What if no one shows up?" I asked after a minute.

"Gerald P. Pinchon's rule number sixteen," Max said calmly. "If you bake it, they will come."

"Okay, so what if they come, stuff their faces, and then leave before I can give them a good reason to vote for me?"

Max shook her head sadly. "Callie, Callie, Callie. Haven't you been paying attention? The food will be reason enough. Take these brownies, for example —" She held the plate under my nose, but yanked it away before I could grab one. "What do you think when you look at them?"

"I think I'm sorry I didn't have a bigger lunch."

Max ignored me. "You think: Warm. Sweet. Happy. Good. After today, when anyone thinks of you, they're going to think of these brownies. They're going to remember how these brownies made them feel. And they're going to think that's how *you* made them feel. And when the time comes, who do you think they're going to vote for? Brianna Blake?" Max wrinkled her nose. "Or warm, sweet, happy, good Callie Singer?"

"Gerald P. Pinchon thinks people are going to vote for me because I'm like a chocolate brownie?" I asked. "Are you sure you didn't take some kind of recipe book out of the library by mistake?"

"Just trust me." The bell rang.

And Max was right: They came.

They came in hungry hordes, lurching toward the table and scooping up armfuls of cookies and Rice Krispie Treats. They came in a storm of handshakes and cheers and yells of, "Good for you, I always thought someone should run against Brianna!" The stream of people turned into a flood, and I stood in the middle of it all, grinning and nodding and trying to remember everyone's names.

I talked to more people in twenty minutes than I'd talked to all year. And, okay, it was kind of hard to tell what they were saying with their mouths stuffed, but I think some of them even promised to vote for me. I started to wonder whether maybe I could actually win.

That's when the music started. At first, it was just a deep, pounding bass.

BOOM. BOOM. BOOM-BOOM-BOOM.

Drums kicked in.

And a guitar riff.

Then we heard it. A voice we'd heard on the radio a million times. But it didn't sound like the radio. It sounded like . . .

"Look!" someone shouted, pointing across the parking lot. A huge flatbed trailer had pulled up to the curb. It was painted fuchsia and covered with flashing neon lights that spelled out PARADISE.

The crowd started to buzz.

"Is it actually her?"

"What would *she* be doing *here*?"

"It *looks* like her, and it *sounds* like her —"

"It can't be!"

But it was.

"Hello, Susan B. Anthony Middle School!" Paradise Patten, teen pop-rock diva, shouted. She waved a pink rhinestone-studded fist at the crowd. "Are you ready to rock?"

"YES!" they shouted in a single, thunderous voice.

Thirty seconds later, I was standing at an empty table, surrounded by empty cupcake wrappers and crumbs. Meanwhile, every kid in school clustered around Paradise's rolling stage, reaching out their arms to try to touch a real, live rock star.

"Before we rock out," Paradise shouted into the mike, "I've got a message for you."

That's when Brianna Blake climbed up onto the trailer bed. Paradise Patten swung an arm around her shoulder. They looked like Rock Star Barbie and her little sister, Wannabe Skipper. "I want you all to vote for my girl here, Brianna Blake, for class council president."

The crowd cheered.

"What are you going to do?" Paradise asked, then held the microphone out to the crowd.

"Vote for Brianna!" they shouted, like trained seals.

"What's that?" she asked again, cupping a hand to her ear. "I can't hear you."

"VOTE FOR BRIANNA! VOTE FOR BRIANNA! VOTE FOR BRIANNA!"

I climbed down off my bench and joined Max. She gave me a sour look. "Brianna Blake's dad is some kind of entertainment lawyer, isn't he?"

I nodded.

"You think Paradise Patten's one of his clients?" she asked.

"What do you think?" I grunted. Then I dropped

my head into my hands. "So I guess this is how it feels to be totally and utterly destroyed by the competition."

Max patted me on the back. "Don't give up hope. We'll think of something else."

"We will?" I asked skeptically. "What?"

Max, the girl with all the answers, had nothing to say. So we just stood there without talking, listening to Brianna's new BFF sing her hit single, "Be My Baby, Baby."

"Want to go over there?" Max asked after a few minutes.

"No way," I said, even though I kind of did. Not that I like that kind of music. Paradise Patten's way too blond and pink and perky for me. But she was still a rock star. And she was singing in the parking lot of *my* middle school. Even I had to admit that was kind of cool. Of course it would make everyone want to vote for Brianna. It almost made *me* want to vote for Brianna. "You want to?"

"No," Max said quickly, though I could tell she kind of did, too.

We didn't move.

"Now here's a new one," Paradise said, pausing while her fans cheered and applauded. "In honor of your soon-to-be president, Brianna Blake!"

Max made a retching noise.

I felt like retching for real.

"She's the one, she's a star!" Paradise sang. A spotlight shone on Brianna, glinting off her platinum hair.

"Vote for her, you'll go far!
All the girls
In all the world,
Want to be like
This super girl."

"I don't believe this," I muttered, praying for a mute button. Or earplugs.

"At least it can't get any worse," Max said.

But then Brianna took the mike.

"I'm the one that can't be beat!" Brianna screeched. Her voice sounded like a drowning cat. It was kind of a relief to know there was at least one thing that Brianna couldn't do perfectly. Her new fans didn't seem to notice.

"Vote Brianna, feel the heat!"

The song went on forever. And by the time they got through the fourth verse, everyone was singing along to the chorus.

"All the girls
In all the world,
Want to be like
This super girl."

57

I was pretty sure I'd be hearing the song in my nightmares that night. Or maybe I was already in the middle of one.

By the time Fish finally wandered over to our table, I wasn't in the best mood.

"Tell me you saved me a chocolate chip cookie?" he shouted over the music. "Let me have two, and I'll be your best friend."

"Are you kidding me?" Max looked like she would have mashed a brownie in his face — if there had been any left.

"Okay, so I already *am* your best friend," Fish admitted. He dropped to his knees. "Does that mean you're going to make me beg?" he asked with a melodramatic whimper. "Please, puh-leeze, all I ask of you is a single cookie. Or two. Or six."

Max looked sick. "How can you still have an appetite after listening to that?" She jerked her head toward the Paradise-mobile.

Fish climbed back to his feet and pulled an iPod out of his pocket. "Who said I was listening?"

That's weird, I thought. Fish didn't own an iPod. Sometimes he borrowed his older brother's, but only after he'd begged and pleaded and vowed to do the dishes for the next two weeks. Which he only did for special occasions. Mobile music emergencies.

The Brianna Show definitely qualified. But how would he have known ahead of time, unless . . . I narrowed my eyes. "Did Brianna tell you she was going to do this?"

Fish dipped his finger into one of the Tupperware containers and scooped out a smear of chocolate frosting. "I guess," he said, licking the chocolate off his finger. "I'm on her campaign team, aren't I?"

I couldn't believe it. "You *knew*, and you let me come out here, anyway, like an idiot? Knowing she was going to do . . ." I couldn't even say it out loud. So I just pointed. *"That?"*

Fish nodded.

"And you didn't *warn* us?" Max asked, incredulous.

"Hey, you're the ones who started all this campaign secrecy stuff," Fish pointed out. "I'm just going along with it. You guys don't want Brianna to know what you're up to — you think she wants you to know what she's planning, either?"

"It's different!" I sputtered.

"Why?"

"Because you're — because —" It was different because Fish was supposed to be *my* best friend, not Brianna's anything. But if he didn't already know that, I definitely wasn't going to tell him. "It doesn't matter," I said instead. "Forget it."

"I don't even know what I'm forgetting," Fish said, laughing. "Girls are so confusing."

"Yeah." I kicked at a loose pebble in the gravel. "We're mysterious creatures. Scientists should study our every move."

Fish laughed again, and I started to feel a little better. No matter what else was happening, I could always make Fish laugh. I was sure Brianna Blake couldn't do that. "Hey, you guys want to forget all this campaign stuff for a while?" I suggested. "*Some* of us still haven't had dessert —" I shot Max an evil grin. "How about milk shakes?"

"Sorry," Fish said. "I've got to meet up with Brianna, Britney, and Ashton after the concert. Serious campaign strategy meeting."

"Oh." Hmph.

"Good," Max said quickly. "Callie and I have an important meeting to get to ourselves."

"We do?" Last I'd heard, Max and I weren't doing anything after the campaign rally but scarfing pizza and watching cheesy movies.

She pressed her lips together tightly and nodded. "We do. And we're late." She grabbed my arm and dragged me away from Fish before either of us could say anything else. Which was probably a good thing, since there was really nothing left to say.

"Do we really have a meeting?" I asked as Max dragged me back toward the main building. "Or were you just saying that?"

"We really do," Max assured me. "A bunch of them, actually." She was walking so fast I almost had to jog to keep up. Max never walks fast. This is a girl whose philosophy of life is "Why run when you can walk?" and, better yet, "Why walk when you can ride?"

"So why don't I know about these meetings?" I asked.

"You're the candidate," Max said lightly. "You've got other things on your mind. That's what I'm here for, to keep track of this kind of thing."

"Uh-huh . . . So what's the real reason?"

She didn't say anything. I stopped walking.

After a few steps, Max realized I wasn't behind her and turned back. She took a deep breath. "I wasn't sure you'd go for it," she admitted.

"Go for what?"

"You'll see. Just remember, Brianna's got celebrities on her side. She's got the whole school thinking she's best friends with Paradise Patten. All we've got are brownies."

"You said brownies were all we needed!"

"That's when I thought Brianna was tuna fish."

Max shook her head, like she was annoyed with herself for getting it wrong. "Brownies always beat tuna fish. But it turns out that Brianna's actually seven-layer death-by-chocolate cake. Brownies just aren't going to get the job done."

I wrinkled my nose. "First of all, I don't know what you're talking about," I said. "And second of all, have I mentioned that I am *starving*? You're not helping."

"All I'm saying is that posters and snacks aren't going to be enough," Max said. "Not if you want to win. Do you want to win?"

"Of course I want to win!" In one afternoon, Brianna had managed to steal my spotlight *and* my best friend. I wasn't about to let her steal the election.

"Then hurry up," she urged me.

"Why? Places to go, people to see?" I teased.

She nodded firmly. "And an election to win."

☆ CHAPTER FIVE ☆

A pale face loomed in the darkness.

His eyes were hooded in shadows.

His hair, black as ink, made it impossible to tell where he ended and the darkness began.

And his voice . . .

He spoke in a low, croaking whisper. "This is what I need from you," he intoned.

"Do we have to do this in the dark?" I complained.

"It adds atmosphere," Max said.

"It's making my eyes hurt." I flipped on the light.

Mr. Hamilton's classroom was empty, except for me, Max, and the pale face floating across from me — which I now saw was attached to an even paler body.

"Terrence Oakley?" I said in surprise.

Terrence bowed as well as he could while still sitting down. "At your service." His voice cracked falsetto on *service*. He didn't even flinch.

"Why am I meeting with Terrence Oakley?" I whispered to Max. She was standing by my shoulder. Even though there were plenty of other seats in the room, she'd insisted that I sit in Mr. Hamilton's chair, behind his big desk, while she stood behind me. Gerald P. Pinchon's rule number five: The appearance of authority *is* authority.

Terrence cleared his throat. "The Society for Investigation of Medieval Warrior Tradition is prepared to —"

"The society for *what*?" I asked.

Max bent down to whisper in my ear. "You know those guys who hang out in the computer lab after school every afternoon playing Legends of the Dragon's Lair?"

I nodded.

"He's their leader. Also known as" — she checked her clipboard — "the Grand Mage of the Middleton Elven Clan, Magician, Second Class. But you can address him as 'Your Honorable Self' or 'O Wise One.'"

I sighed. "What do you want, Terrence?"

"As I was saying, the Society is prepared to offer

you our support in the upcoming election, pro-
vided you're able to make us the following
promises." He pulled out a graphing calculator and
began scrolling down the screen. "One: Convince
the administration to purchase new computers,
preferably models with a Nitro 17 processor and a
hi-res VDU with TFT LCD. Two: Institute a behavior
code distributing punitive measures to anyone
who insists on referring to members of the Society
by derogatory terms such as *nerd*, *geek*, *dragon
food*, et cetera, et cetera. Three —"

"Terrence," I jumped in, "I'm not really sure the
class council president can —"

"We can't promise to do any of those things,"
Max said flatly.

"Then what am I doing here?" Terrence asked.

"I said we can't *promise*," Max said. "That
doesn't mean we can't try."

Terrence scowled. "And you want me to vote
for Callie based on *trying*? Anyone can try. *Brianna*
can try. My people want action."

Max shook her head. "You're absolutely right,"
she said. "Brianna *could* try . . . but will she?"

"What's that supposed to mean?" Terrence
asked.

"It means, Brianna's been class council president for years, right?"

Terrence nodded.

"And in all those years, how many meetings has she had with you? How many of your problems has she solved? How many times has she promised to try to help you with *anything*?"

Terrence held up his hand, his fingers curled into a circle.

Zero.

"And how many times has she walked past you in the halls without even noticing you, or worse, calling you by the wrong name?"

"So many times it would take the Nitro 17 processor twenty years to count them all up," Terrence admitted.

"So aren't you tired of it?" Max asked. "Don't you want someone who will listen to your problems? Don't you want someone who remembers your name? Don't you want someone who cares enough to *try*?"

"I guess." Terrence shifted in his chair. "Yeah. Yeah, I do!" His voice squeaked again.

I had to hand it to Max. She was brilliant.

"How many demands do you have on that list of yours, O Wise One?" Max asked.

"Twelve."

Max tapped her pen against her clipboard.

"Okay, here's what we're going to do. You're going to walk us through each item on the list, and explain to Callie exactly what your problem is and how we can help you fix it. We've got a lot of people to see this afternoon, but we're going to sit here as long as it takes, because we want to know what we can do for *you*. Don't we, Callie?"

It took me a moment to realize it was my turn to speak. "Oh, um. Yes. Sure. We want to know."

And so he told us *everything*. Terrence talked for almost half an hour, without pausing for breath. It was like no one had ever listened to him before. And okay, I guess I can see why. Let's just say that I now know more about digital dragon-slaying than I ever wanted to. A lot more. But it wasn't all snooze-worthy. Some of what he was saying actually made sense. *The lab* does *need new computers,* I realized. *And maybe if I were president* — but I stopped myself there. Before I could do anything to help anyone, I had to win the election. And after the whole Paradise parking-lot disaster, there wasn't much chance of that.

Finally, Terrence ran out of things to complain about.

"Only one promise," Max reminded him. "We promise to *try*. And that's *if* we get elected."

Terrence folded up his list of demands and handed it to her. "That's all the promise I need."

Max tucked his paper into her clipboard. "So we have your support on election day?"

He nodded. "You have my word as a mage and a dragon slayer. The Society will support you."

Max smiled. "You've made the right decision."

"Max, you want to explain to me why we sat through all that?" I asked, once Terrence had scuttled out of the room.

She shrugged. "We can't make promises we can't deliver on, right? But the important thing is that no one with any power has *ever* listened to Terrence Oakley. No one except Callie Singer. You're the candidate who listens, the candidate who tries. The candidate who cares . . . or at least pretends to care. This is how we're going to win."

"The Society for . . . whatever is going to get me elected?" I asked skeptically. "All six of them?"

Max raised her eyebrows. "There are eight of them. But Callie, this is just the beginning. Gerald P. Pinchon's rule number four: Bricks are small. But buildings are large."

"I get what you're saying," I admitted. "But do you really think there are enough people waiting out in that hallway to vote me into office? Just because I pretend to care about their problems, you think they'll vote against Brianna?"

"Callie, how many things do you hate about this school?"

"I don't *hate* anything," I reminded her.

"Okay — how many things do you loathe and detest?"

"And abhor," I said. "Don't forget abhor. That's the best one."

"A lot, right? Cafeteria food, crowded stairways, gym class —"

"Stop right there," I begged. "Now you're just depressing me."

"Here's why we're going to win," Max said. "This school only has one Brianna Blake. But it has a *lot* of Callie Singers."

"Thanks a lot!" I protested. "So now you're saying I'm just like everyone else?"

Max patted me on the shoulder. "Of course you're special," she teased, in a sugary-sweet kindergarten teacher's voice. "You're special and unique and wonderful and —"

I shrugged her off. "Enough, you're making my teeth hurt."

"As I was saying," Max said, grinning at me, "this school is full of Callie Singers. It's full of people who have a ton to complain about and no one to listen. *Brianna's* certainly not going to. *You* will."

"Sounds like fun," I grumbled.

"Sounds like a winning strategy. And we're just getting started." She put down the clipboard and stuck her head outside the classroom door. "Next!"

"You sure about this?" I asked, pausing at the door of Cosmo's Pizza later that afternoon.

We never went to Cosmo's. It wasn't for people like us. It was for the popular kids. I'd never been inside before, and I almost expected an invisible force field to block my way, or an alarm to sound when I stepped through the door. Flashing lights, a howling siren, and a spotlight aimed at my face. Just so everyone there would know I didn't belong. Like it wasn't already obvious.

"Definitely," Max said. "I'm hungry, and we're here. Let's do it."

I wasn't surprised she was hungry. Max had been working hard all afternoon, fooling half the kids in school into believing we cared about their problems.

The president of the chess team wanted money to attend an international junior chess tournament in the Ukraine.

Two delegates from the model rocket-building club wanted permission to build a full-scale planetary orbiter in the football field.

The trumpet section of the marching band had played an off-key version of the school alma mater for us, then demanded new uniforms, new instruments, and, once a month, a halftime show extended to the length of a football game.

The ballroom dance society wanted the floors of the gym refinished. The juggling club wanted permission to play with fire. The bowling team wanted personalized balls. The math squad wanted leather jackets.

Everyone wanted something. And I had to admit, Max was good. She had them all buying her act. I almost bought it myself. So when we'd finally managed to clear them out, and Max asked me for a favor, I couldn't say no. Not after she'd worked so hard all afternoon. That is, I couldn't say no until I found out the favor was a trip to Cosmo's. Then I said it immediately.

And I kept saying it, right up until the moment Max opened the door and stepped inside. I took a deep breath, and followed.

There was no alarm.

No flashing light.

No siren.

Just an ordinary pizza place with checkered tablecloths, plastic cloves of garlic hanging from the ceiling, and clusters of popular kids huddled around every table. I told myself they weren't all staring at me, wondering what I was doing there.

But it really felt like they were.

Wait. That wasn't my imagination. One of the groups *was* staring at me.

"Callie!" someone shouted, waving. "Callie, come sit over here!"

I couldn't believe it. It was Jackson Cummings, star pitcher, all-star MVP, and all-around jerk. Jackson Cummings, who had dunked me nine times at last year's winter carnival.

"You think it's some kind of joke?" I asked Max, narrowing my eyes.

"I think we should go sit down before they change their minds," Max said.

Jackson was sharing a pizza with Marcus Clark, Gary Plenum, and Carl "The Refrigerator" Joseph. They were all jocks, they were all more than six feet tall already, and they were all the most popular guys in school. None of them had spoken to me since fourth grade.

"You want to share a table with *them*?" I whispered to Max. "Weren't you just saying that the sum of all their IQs was probably smaller than your shoe size? And that Gary Plenum eats like a trash compactor?"

"You make it sound mean," Max said, flushing. "I was just joking. And besides, you were the one who said Marcus Clark smells like a skunk."

"He *does*!" I pointed out. "Which is exactly my point. Why would we sit with them?"

"Because nothing goes better with greasy pizza than a delicious bouquet of skunk stink?" Max suggested, grinning. And, before I could protest, she dragged me toward the table and pulled me down into the booth.

"Callie Singer!" Carl shouted like I was across the restaurant rather than squished into the red leather booth right next to him.

Gary slapped me on the back, hard. "So great to see you, *Callie Singer*! Your rally was awesome today!"

"Yeah!" Jackson agreed. "Those brownies were sweet! You're the greatest, *Callie Singer*!"

"Why are they yelling?" I whispered to Max. "And why do they keep shouting my name?"

She shrugged.

"Dude, you want some pizza?" Jackson asked. "It's *awesome*."

"Um, sure?" I took a piece of pizza — piled high

with mushrooms, pepperoni, onions, and sausage, but no anchovies — and started nibbling at the edge.

"Dude, did you see Callahan at practice?" Marcus asked his friends.

"Dude was a total spaz-machine," Gary said.

"*You're* a spaz-machine," Jackson countered.

"Dude, you want me to cram this pizza in your face?" Gary asked.

"You know what I want?" Jackson asked.

There was a pause.

Then Jackson stuck his fist under his armpit, and flapped his arm down like a chicken. It made the kind of revolting noise you would expect.

Marcus started laughing so hard, soda spurted out of his nose.

"Dude, soda just came out of your nose!" Carl shouted, laughing and pointing.

Then they all tried it.

Max scrunched her eyebrows together and cupped a hand around her mouth. *"Smells like skunk,"* she mouthed, giving me a wicked grin. I choked back a giggle. *So this is how the popular kids spend their time*, I thought. *At least now I know what I've been missing. Not much.*

Something wet spattered against my forehead. It dripped down my face.

"Uh, dude, sorry, Callie," Jackson said, wiping his nose with his fist.

Jackson had dunked me again.

"I'm just going to go get some napkins," I muttered. The boys didn't notice. They were too busy trying to see if Gary could stuff a whole slice of pizza into his mouth at once. I slid out of the booth. Max jumped up and followed me. We burst into laughter as soon as we were safely hidden behind the napkin dispenser.

"Unbelievable," I sputtered, wiping a wad of napkins across my sticky forehead.

"Un*believable*," Max agreed. "And Marcus really does smell like —"

"Stop!" I shook my head, trying to catch my breath. "If you say it again, I'll never stop laughing. I can't believe you said it while we were sitting right there! I thought I was going to spit out my soda."

Max giggled. "You would have fit right in."

"Lucky me," I said. "I think I'd rather fit into the monkey cage at the zoo."

Max raised her eyebrows. "Same difference, right?"

After I finally managed to swallow the rest of my laughter, I grabbed a few more napkins for my forehead. But it was going to take a lot more than napkins to wipe off that grossness. "Come on, let's go."

The smile dropped off Max's face. "Go where?"

"Uh, home? Also known as a land far, far away from the soda-snorting doofuses?"

She grabbed my arm. "You can't!"

I shook her off. "What's with you? Are you saying you want to go back there and sit down again? With *them*? Very funny. But seriously, let's go."

"Callie, I am serious. You can't."

I took a closer look at Max's face. Her lips were pressed together, and the left corner of her mouth was twitching. I've known her long enough to know what that means. She was up to something. Something that had to do with the fact that the coolest guys in school had mysteriously discovered my existence. "You don't seem very surprised by all this," I said suspiciously.

"Callie, think. Those guys are *cool*. If other people see you hanging out with them, they'll start thinking you're cool, too," she said. "Do you know how many votes this could get us if we stay?"

"But I'm *not* cool, remember? Don't you think people will wonder *why* those guys suddenly want to hang out with me?"

She didn't say anything.

"Max, what did you do?"

"Gerald P. Pinchon's rule number nine: An endorsement from the right person is worth —"

"I didn't ask Gerald P. Pinchon. I asked you. What's going on?"

"I bribed them," she admitted.

"You did *what*?" I shouted. Half the restaurant turned around to stare at me. I knew it had to happen sooner or later.

"Shhh," Max hissed. "Play it cool."

"I don't know *how* to play it cool," I pointed out. "I'm *not* cool, obviously, or you wouldn't have had to *bribe* those guys to hang out with me." I slapped my hands over my face. "This is totally humiliating."

"No, this is politics," Max retorted. "And, FYI, you're way cooler than any of those guys, even if they're too dumb to notice."

"Am not."

"Are too."

"Am not."

Max reached over and pried my hands away from my face. "You. Are. Cool." She faked a haughty Brianna Blake–like voice. "After all, would someone like *me* waste my time with someone like *you* if you weren't cool as ice?"

Mad as I was, I couldn't help smiling. "No offense, Max, but you're about as cool as a volcano."

She raised her eyebrows so high they poked up over the rims of her glasses. "You, on the other hand? Cool as the Arctic Circle post-global-warming."

"As in, icy but melting?"

"Exactly. And those guys?" She pointed back toward our table, where the jocks were taking turns balancing an empty pizza tray on their heads. "They're exactly the patch we need to repair your ozone layer."

I sighed. It was hard to stay mad at Max when she was being so charmingly dorky. It was one of the things I liked best about her — she didn't try to be cool. Which meant, no matter what I told her, she just *was* cool. Even if no one but Fish and I had figured it out yet. "Okay, just tell me. How much did you have to offer them to get them to put up with me?"

"I want to remind you that there are plenty of us crazy enough to put up with you for free," Max said quickly. "And just because they're too dumb to notice that you can — very occasionally — be a little bit awesome, that doesn't mean —"

"Flattery's not going to distract me," I warned her. "What did you offer them?"

"Free brownies every day for two weeks, if they . . . hung out with you here, while everyone's watching. And if they were friendlier to you in school. You know, getting everyone to believe that they, well . . ."

"Don't think I'm a total loser?"

"It's called an endorsement. Like in a commercial, when they get some famous basketball player to talk about how much he loves a certain brand of foot cream —"

"So before I was a brownie, now I'm foot cream?"

"If the jocks love you, everyone will love you," Max said stubbornly. "It's a fact of middle school life. You think anyone in this restaurant thinks for themselves?"

"Maybe not," I said, "but . . ."

Max suddenly pointed behind me. "Hey, Fish is here."

As if I was going to fall for that. "Nice try," I told her. "You know Fish is at some kind of strategy meeting."

Max tipped her head to the side. "It doesn't look like they're doing much strategizing to me."

I turned around.

Fish was squeezed into a booth with Brianna, Britney, and Ashton. He was chowing down on pizza. *I bet it's* anchovy *pizza,* I thought. *Our pizza.* And he was laughing. They were all laughing.

I marched over to their table before I had time to think.

"Hey," I said.

Fish looked up. He didn't even bother to look guilty. "Oh. Uh, hey."

"Hello, Callie," Brianna said sweetly. "How are you? That was such an *adorable* shindig you threw in the parking lot this afternoon. I hope I didn't drown you out with my little performance."

"Oh no," I said, matching her sweetness. Let her be vanilla frosting — I would be maple sugar candy. I'd make her teeth rot. "It was a treat for us all. Really. You should be onstage more often."

Brianna laughed. "Bad idea." She turned to Fish. "Remember that time with the bananas, Jacob?" she asked, then dissolved into ladylike, snort-free giggles. He started laughing, too, until he nearly choked on one of his anchovies. Served him right.

He drew in a deep breath, sputtering out a few more laughs before he got himself under control. "The bananas *and* the monkey song," he added.

Brianna's giggles sounded all tinkly and musical, like someone playing a xylophone. And when she finally stopped, it was only to give me one of her oh-so-superior smiles. "Sorry, Callie. Inside joke."

"Right," I said, forcing every emotion out of my voice. But inside, I was raging. *Inside joke?* Who was Brianna Blake to have an inside joke with *my* best friend?

I waited for Fish to loop me in, but he just shrugged. "Guess you had to be there."

"Actually, I guess I *didn't*," I muttered. "Seems like you're doing fine without me."

"What?"

"Nothing." I didn't want to seem jealous. *Just smile,* I told myself. But I felt more like a wild animal, baring my fangs.

"Callie, I wanted to tell you, I'm just so glad you're running for president, too," Brianna said, and *her* fake smile was a prize winner. "It's going to be so much fun to finally have someone to campaign against."

"Winning without a fight is *so* boring?" Britney said. "When we win this year, it's going to be so much cooler?"

"You mean, *if* you win," Max corrected her, appearing at my side.

"Of course." Brianna took a dainty bite of her pizza. She dabbed her mouth with a napkin, but it was just for show. She was too perfect to have sauce on her face. "*If* we win."

Ashton and Britney started laughing.

Fish stared down at his empty plate.

"We *always* win?" Britney said. "Who would vote against Brianna?"

Fish still said nothing.

I told myself to stay calm. I couldn't let them know that they got to me. Instead, I had to fight fire with fire.

"Come on, Max, we'd better get back to our table. Jackson will be wondering where we went."

Brianna gaped. "Jackson *Cummings*?" she asked. I remembered that Brianna and Jackson used to go out. The rumor was, he broke up with her over the summer for an eighth grader.

"*You're* sitting with Jackson Cummings?" Britney asked, and this time, it was a real question.

I shrugged, like it was no big deal. "Sure," I said. "And Gary and Carl and Marcus. You know, all the guys."

"Right," Ashton said weakly, looking like she was trying to solve a really hard math problem in her head. "All the guys."

"Later!" I called cheerily, and pulled Max away, back toward our table and "our guys."

"I thought you were out of here?" Max asked with a knowing smile.

"And make you bake all those brownies for nothing?" I asked. "I don't think so." I squeezed back into the booth, next to The Refrigerator. "Miss me, guys?" I asked.

"Callie Singer!" they all shouted at once. "You're back!"

"I'm back!" I cried twice as loud. I didn't care if they were dumb jocks, or if they squirted a whole pizza out of their noses. I didn't care if Max was bribing them to hang out with me, or if I had to promise them a whole new baseball stadium to get their vote.

I was going to wipe the smiles off those girls' faces.

I was going to prove to Fish that *I* was the better candidate — *and* the better friend — even if I didn't have shiny blond hair and a big-screen TV.

I was going to beat Brianna Blake. No matter what.

"So," I said heartily, peering around the table, "who wants to bet I can squirt this soda out of my nose *and* cram this whole slice of pizza in my mouth at the same time?"

☆ CHAPTER SIX ☆

After that, things got kind of weird.

As a general rule, no one at Susan B. Anthony cared too much about school elections. But according to Gerald P. Pinchon, rules were made to be broken. (Except his, I guess.)

There were other seventh grade races, of course, not that anyone had noticed. Carla Mathers was running for her third term as class secretary — unopposed. Ellis Coover had the race for treasurer all wrapped up, mostly because no one else wanted the job except Janice Meier, whose idea of campaigning was to carry around a stuffed Scrooge McDuck. No one knew why. The race for vice president might have heated up, if Alex Schaffer hadn't gotten expelled the day after his opponent, Miles

Ang, had eaten a candy bar laced with peanuts, setting off an allergic reaction that would keep him out of school for weeks. And since the other classes all held their elections at different times, Brianna and I had the spotlight to ourselves.

Max and I plastered every wall with posters — but not the normal kind. After the campaign rally fizzled out, we'd thrown out all our glitter.

"We can't out-Brianna Brianna," Max had declared. So we went with Plan B. I would become the anti-Brianna. It seemed like a good idea, since basically, I already was.

We didn't come up with any cheesy slogans or paint my name bright and shiny in neon paint. In fact, most of the posters didn't have my name on them at all — they were just black with white type, and a single word: CHANGE. Others were white with black type: THINK. My favorites were the gray ones that read DID YOU EVER STOP TO THINK . . . YOU MIGHT BE RIGHT? No one was quite sure what they meant, but everyone had an opinion — and according to Max, that was the point.

Then there were the posters that weren't posters at all. We pasted index cards along every hallway, each of them crammed with some bizarre factoid in Max's impossibly neat and tiny handwriting:

THERE ARE EIGHTEEN DIFFERENT ANIMALS IN ANIMAL CRACKERS: TIGERS, COUGARS, CAMELS, RHINOCEROSES, KANGAROOS, HIPPOPOTAMUSES, BISON, LIONS, HYENAS, ZEBRAS, ELEPHANTS, SHEEP, BEARS, GORILLAS, MONKEYS, SEALS, AND GIRAFFES. VOTE CALLIE SINGER.

WHEN YOU'RE WITHIN THE BOUNDARIES OF THE STATE OF ARKANSAS, IT IS ILLEGAL TO MISPRONOUNCE THE WORD "ARKANSAS." VOTE CALLIE SINGER.

YOU WILL EAT 60,000 POUNDS OF FOOD IN YOUR LIFETIME. THAT IS THE WEIGHT OF SIX ELEPHANTS. OR 170,000 IPODS. VOTE CALLIE SINGER.

"I don't get it," I'd told Max. "What does me getting elected have to do with the state of Arkansas? Or the world's oldest piece of chewing gum? Or the number of insect pieces allowed in a candy bar?" (According to Max, it was seven. Guess who's never eating a candy bar *ever* again?)

"Nothing," Max said. "And everything. This isn't about getting people to vote for you — it's about getting people to notice you. We want them to realize that this election isn't like every other year, and you're not like every other candidate."

"Every other candidate? What other candidate has there ever been, except Brianna Blake?"

"Exactly. So we run the campaign that Brianna Blake *never* would."

There was just one problem: We weren't the only candidate running the campaign that Brianna Blake never would. Brianna was, too.

Sure, she stuck up the same pink posters she used every year. They were showered with glitter, and crammed with the same old cheesy slogans. But then there were the other posters: Fish's posters. They weren't just different. They were amazing.

He'd used white pastels on black poster board. At first, it just seemed like a mess of swirls and curls and lines — and then you blinked, and it was Brianna's face. It looked exactly like her, but somehow *better* than her, dramatic and wild and retro and futuristic all at the same time. The halls may have been crammed with posters, but those jumped out at you. No one could help staring as they walked by, even me. Fish really was an incredible artist, I thought.

Too bad he was working for the enemy.

I figured people would just ignore the posters and all the campaign stuff like they did every year, but I figured wrong. Everywhere I went, people wanted to talk to me about the election, promising to vote for me. It happened in math class, in the cafeteria, even once at the mall. I felt like a celebrity.

In the second week of the campaign, Brianna handed out armbands to all her supporters. They were pink and emblazoned with a glittery silver *B*. Brianna wore one herself. And since everything Brianna wore automatically became fashion-able, there were suddenly armbands everywhere we looked.

Until the next day, when Max brought in a bag of black headbands. They weren't stylish, they weren't expensive, they didn't have a glittery *C* anywhere on them. They were just the kind you can get at the sporting goods store, fifty for five dollars. But everyone knew what they meant — and almost everyone wanted one. *Everyone.*

Picture this: Wednesday morning gym class, awful as always. In fact, worse than awful, because we were still slogging through our softball unit, and this time, there was no escape. I was up to bat in the fifth inning. We were down two outs. Which, if I understood the rules correctly — doubtful — meant it was up to me. I didn't get sports in general, and I *really* didn't get softball. But I got that the whole game was riding on me. I also got plenty of nasty looks from the pink-armbanded girls fluttering around Brianna in the dugout, who knew that I was destined to strike out. As always. They may have been on my team, but they definitely weren't on my side. I hunched over home plate, gripping the bat and praying that the ball would hit me in the face, since a walk was the only way I'd ever get to first base.

Ms. Soderberg glared at me from the pitcher's mound. She narrowed her eyes. Wiped the sweat off her forehead. (Ms. Soderberg layered up in purple sweats to shield herself from the almost-winter wind. Most Wednesdays, she looked like an eggplant — and spurted sweat like a water fountain.) I dug in behind the plate. Took a deep breath, and —

The ball flew wildly off course, dropping to the ground three feet from home plate and rolling toward the parking lot.

Ball one.

Ms. Soderberg wiped more sweat out of her eyes. Wound up. Pitched. It flew hard and fast and I prepared myself to swing, but then —

Ball two.

"Excuse me, Ms. Soderberg?" Max shouted from the safety of the dugout.

I couldn't believe it. Max and I had a very strict set of survival rules for gym class, and number one was: Be seen, but not heard. (And when at all possible, don't be seen, either.)

Ms. Soderberg grunted. Max took it as an

invitation. She hopped out of the dugout and ran across the field, clutching something black in her fist.

No way, I thought, even though I was pretty sure I knew exactly what it was. *Not possible. She wouldn't.*

But she would. She did.

And when she ran back to the dugout, her hand was empty. The black headband was back at the pitcher's mound, wrapped around Ms. Soderberg's head. Keeping the sweat out of her eyes — and announcing to the whole world that she was one of my biggest fans.

Even if she didn't know it. Max was brilliant.

"Ready, Singer?" Ms. Soderberg shouted, adjusting the headband. I glanced over my shoulder at Brianna and her pink-armbanded flock. They didn't look happy.

"Is your arm cold, Ms. Soderberg?" Britney called out, waving her armband in the air. "This will keep you warm?"

"Forget about the weather, girls!" Ms. Soderberg called back. "Focus on the game!"

Britney jumped out of the dugout, ran halfway toward the pitcher's mound, then stopped midfield, looking like she couldn't remember where she'd been going. "But you don't understand?" she asked. "Brianna needs you?"

"Your *team* needs you," Ms. Soderberg snapped. "They need you to stop distracting them. Twenty laps!"

"What?"

"You heard me. Twenty laps, Britney. That should warm your arms right up."

Britney opened her mouth — then shut it again. She trotted over to the track and began to run. It was, officially, the best Wednesday of my life.

"Let's go, Singer!" Ms. Soderberg shouted.

"Ready!" I called back. And I was. For the first time in the history of gym class, I was ready. Britney was dragging herself around the track. Brianna was in the corner of the dugout, sulking. Ms. Soderberg was advertising for my campaign without even knowing it. Obviously, the universe was on my side.

My hands tightened around the bat. This was it, I decided. If I was ever going to hit the ball, it would be today. I could already hear the crack of the bat against the ball, feel the moment of impact, see the ball sailing up, up, and away, over Ms. Soderberg's head, over the bases, over the outfielders trying their best to be invisible, over the fence. I could hear the cheers as I rounded the bases and slid into home. I could —

"Strike one!" Ms. Soderberg shouted, as the ball whizzed by me. "Next time, try swinging!"

And the next time, I did. That was strike two.

That made sense, I decided. In the movies, the hero never hit the home run until the very last pitch. It was all much more exciting and dramatic that way. So this final pitch, this would be it. Ms. Soderberg wound up and tossed the ball. I swung as hard as I could, and . . .

Strike three.

That was it. No home run. No wild cheers or inspirational music played over the closing credits. Not even a fly ball that would give me a five-second thrill before someone made an easy catch and sent me shuffling back to the dugout. Just three strikes and I was out.

But I couldn't have cared less. Britney was still jogging around the track. (Not that it was much of a jog — I'd seen her do faster laps around the mall). Brianna was still sulking. And, best of all, Ms. Soderberg was still wearing the black headband. *My* black headband.

Who cares about being a softball hero? I thought as I joined my team back on the field, snagging my favorite spot behind — *way* behind — second base. *I'm going to be a* president.

Three strikes or not, it was still officially the best Wednesday in history — and it was just beginning. That day, black was the opposite of pink, just like I was the opposite of Brianna. And when I walked through the halls, a sea of black-headbanded heads bobbed past me, grinning and cheering whenever they spotted my face. I was famous.

More than that, I was *popular.*

Maybe people suddenly cared about whether we raised money with a carnival, a bake sale, a dance-a-thon, or a knitting bee. Maybe more people than I thought actually cared about what happened at class council meetings, or knew what the class council even did.

But I didn't think so.

This wasn't about the election, not really. It wasn't even about me and Brianna. It was about the way people like her always won without even trying. It was about people like me deciding to put up a fight. And apparently, Max was right: There were more people like me than I'd thought.

"One person, one vote," Max kept saying. "And the uncool kids outnumber the cool ones. Majority rules."

The math was simple. So simple, even Britney and Ashton could have done it. If it all came down to us versus them, then we were unbeatable. Because *they* were popular. *They* were elite. Not just anyone could be *them*. That's what made them special.

And that's why there were a whole lot more of *us*.

One person, one vote. No one's special inside the voting booth. On election day, the only special one is the winner.

And I was starting to think it could be me.

The lunchtime poll was Max's idea. By which I mean, it was Gerald P. Pinchon's idea. Rule number three: Give the people what they want. According to Max, that one went along with rule number eight: Always know what the people want. So Max went out into the wild — otherwise known as the cafeteria — to find out. I waited in the second-floor bathroom for her to show up with the results. It wasn't an easy wait, and not just because the bathroom smelled worse than my brother. I actually wanted to find out what the rest of the seventh grade thought of me. Was I really presidential material?

"Yes!" Max cried as she slipped into the bathroom, wedging the door shut behind her with a rubber doorstop.

"Yes?" I repeated. "You mean —"

"I mean, *yes*!" She pumped her fist in the air. "We're really doing this." Max pulled out her clipboard, jabbing her finger at each bullet point she ran through. "Fifty-two percent believe you're the right person for the job. Fifty-four percent like what you stand for. Forty-nine percent are impressed by your campaign. And, if the election were held today, twelve percent are undecided, forty-three percent would vote for Brianna, and forty-*five* percent would vote for you. Which I think calls for another *yes!*"

"Forty-five percent?" I said. "Forty-five for me and forty-three for Brianna? That doesn't sound very . . . certain."

Max shook her head. "Don't you get it? At the beginning of this election, *no one* would have voted for you. Look how far we've come! We've pulled even with Brianna, and if the election were held today, you'd probably win. Maybe by only one or two votes, but that's all you need. And this is just phase one!"

I could win, I thought, trying to make the words make sense. *I could actually win.*

"So what's phase two?" I asked.

"Phase one was getting people to notice you and your campaign," Max explained. "We wanted to get them talking. Now we want to get them voting. For *you*. Which means figuring out what kind of candidate they want you to be."

"Gerald P. Pinchon's rules number eight and ten," I said proudly.

Max raised her eyebrows. "Don't tell me you've actually started *listening* to me? Are you feeling feverish? Delirious?"

"More like insane," I said. "But since me running for president is totally crazy, anyway, I figure I might as well go all the way. So —" I took a deep breath, trying to prepare myself. Criticism is *not* my favorite thing. Let's just say that on the list of things I don't hate, it ranks somewhere between gym class and liverwurst. "Tell me what's wrong with me. What do I need to change?"

"You're looking at this all wrong," Max said. "It's not about what's *wrong* with you. It's just about high-lighting the positive. Finding out what people think is right, and keeping their focus on that. Distracting them from things that . . . aren't so right."

"Uh-huh. Sure. So what's un-right? Come on, I can take it." After all, how bad could it be? Especially on the best Wednesday of my life?

"Well . . ." Max peered down at her clipboard. She bit down on a thumbnail and began to slowly gnaw off the tip. Totally gross — but totally Max. "It's possible you could be more, um, friendly."

"I *am* friendly!" I protested. "Aren't I friendly to you?"

Max grinned, but didn't say anything.

I wadded up a length of toilet paper and threw it at her. She swatted it away. "Now, how is that friendly?" she teased.

"I'm serious!"

"So am I," she said. "It's not about being friendly to me, it's about being friendly to other people —"

I opened my mouth, but she cut me off before I could argue.

"*All* people," she said sternly. "Even the ones you think are annoying. Or idiotic. Or rude. Or weird."

"That's a lot of people," I said doubtfully.

"That's kind of my point," Max said.

I nodded firmly. "Okay. Friendly. I can do that. I *should* do that, right? It'll make me a better person or something."

"Exactly."

That wasn't so bad. "Next?" I asked.

Max squinted at her list. "I guess you could, well, smile more. No more frowning."

"What frowning?"

"You're frowning right now!" she said accusingly.

I looked in the mirror. That was just the way my mouth was. I forced it up into a crazy clown smile. "This better?" I asked, gritting my teeth.

Max didn't laugh. "I hate to say it, but that's perfect. You want to know the truth?"

"I'm not sure," I said.

"If you want to win, you should probably start smiling like that all the time. Act happy, no matter how you're feeling. No more negative comments, no more complaints, no more talking about what's wrong with the school. Focus on what's *right* with the school. People want a president who's sunny and cheerful."

"Hold on," I protested. "*Brianna*'s the sunny and cheerful one. I'm the anti-Brianna. Doesn't that mean I get to be as gloom and doom as I want to be?"

"Anti-Brianna was okay for a start," Max admitted. "But attitude counts. People want a president who they think would be fun to hang out with."

"Don't people want a president who will do a good job of running the school?"

Max rolled her eyes. "I wish. But in the real world, people don't vote the issues. When you get down to it, life is a popularity contest. And Brianna is, well . . ."

"Popular," I said sourly.

"I didn't make it up," Max said. She tapped her clipboard. "It's right here in black and white. People think of you as kind of cranky. It's a stupid reason not to vote for someone — but it's still a reason. And we don't want to give them any reasons at all."

"So you think I should turn myself into Brianna Blake?" I knew I was frowning, but I couldn't care less.

"No way!" Max cried. "*No* election is worth that. I'm just saying, you could smile more. You don't have to express every single emotion you have, you know? You don't have to tell the whole truth and nothing but the truth every minute of every day."

"Speaking of the whole truth and nothing but the truth . . ." I peered over at her clipboard. "What's all that stuff in the middle there that you skipped over?"

"What?" she asked innocently.

I tried to read upside down, but the letters swam across the page. "In between 'be friendlier' and 'smile more,'" I said, pointing at the long list in the middle of the two big bullet points. "What else did people say about me?"

"Nothing you need to worry about," she said quickly, pulling the clipboard away. "Just do those two things, and I think we've really got a shot."

"Max!"

She shifted her weight from one foot to the other. She fiddled with the earpiece of her glasses. She tapped her pen against the clipboard. And she did everything she could not to look me in the eye.

Here's the thing about Max: She's a terrible liar. It's not because she's too goody-goody to ever tell a little white lie — trust me, she tries. She's just not good at it. When she's got a piece of information, she can't stand to keep it shut up inside of her. No matter how hard she tries to hold it in, it ends up dribbling out around the edges. Like now.

I grabbed the clipboard out of her hands and flipped back to the poll results. It wasn't pretty.

And, according to the poll, neither was I.

"Six percent think my jeans don't fit right," I read. "Nine percent think my hair would look better parted on the other side. *Twelve percent* think I should be wearing lip gloss?" I looked up at Max in disbelief. "Twelve percent of the people in this school are paying attention to what color my mouth is?"

Max grabbed the clipboard back. "I told you not to look. It's ridiculous."

"It *is* ridiculous," I agreed. "But . . . you took this poll for a reason, right?"

"To find out what the people want," Max said. "That doesn't mean we have to give it to them."

"Gerald P. Pinchon would say we do," I pointed out.

"You hate makeup," Max protested. "You cut your own hair. Do you really want to change all that, just to win an election?"

"Want to? No. But if I'm going to beat Brianna, maybe I have to beat her at her own game."

Max looked skeptical. "Are you sure?"

I glanced in the mirror. My hair was sticking out in all directions because I'd gotten up too late to brush it that morning. My T-shirt was black with bright green patches sewn on the shoulder to cover up where I'd ripped it, and totally wrinkled because it had been sitting on the floor of my closet since last spring. My face was makeup-free and frowny — just the way I liked it. I looked like Callie Singer — just the way I liked *me*.

But that didn't mean everyone else liked me that way. And if I was going to beat Brianna, I had to get them on my side.

"I'm sure."

Max beamed, then opened her backpack and pulled out a bulky plastic bag. She dumped out the contents, and a whole drugstore's worth of makeup clattered out onto the counter. "Then we'd better get started. We have got a lot of work to do."

"Wait a second," I said. "You weren't even going to tell me what the poll said, but you just happened to be walking around with all that makeup?"

Max looked the same way she did that time I found her leafing through the encyclopedia when she'd said she was going to be watching cartoons. Caught. She cleared her throat. "Always be prepared, right? This was *your* idea," she added when she realized I was hesitating. "Okay, so I bought the makeup, but I'd never make you turn yourself into someone you didn't want to be. But if *you* want to . . ."

I sighed. "You really think you can give me a makeover?" I asked. "You're not exactly a makeup expert, you know." Max hated makeup even more than I did. Which was a lot. She just didn't care what anyone else thought about how she looked — as long as she liked it, she was happy. It had always been one of the things we had in common. Until now.

"Whether or not I wear makeup is irrelevant," Max assured me. "I've done plenty of research on what's in and what's out, and I know exactly what we need to do to make you look like the perfect candidate." She pointed at the bathroom counter. "Sit."

I wrinkled my nose. "You want me to sit on *that*? Gross."

"You don't have to lick it, just sit on it."

I sat.

She grabbed a brush in one hand and a compact filled with some kind of pink powder in the other. I cringed, but forced myself to hold still.

"You ready for the new Callie Singer?" Max asked, waving the brush toward my cheeks.

I glanced over my shoulder, catching one last glimpse of the old Callie Singer in the spotted mirror.

It's just temporary, I told myself, *until the election. And it's only my face — it's not like I'm changing who I* am.

"Close your eyes," Max instructed. "This won't hurt. And it'll be over before you know it."

It was exactly the same thing Dr. Saperstein always said, right before he pulled out a massive needle and gave me a shot. And I believed Max just as much as I always believed him.

Meaning: not a single bit.

"What did you do to your *face*?" Fish exclaimed when I opened the front door that night. We were supposed to be working on our extra-credit report for social studies. It was the first time we'd hung out in days.

I'm going to kill Max, I thought, wiping the back of my hand across my mouth to try to smear off some of the pink gloss. I hadn't had time to wash off any of the makeup before meeting up with Fish — and Max had insisted that it would make a good test run. Of course, Max had also promised that I didn't look like a total freak.

Maybe she was a better liar than I'd thought.

"What's wrong with it?" I asked Fish.

"Nothing's . . . wrong," he said hesitantly. "It's just — wait, are you wearing *lipstick*?"

"Gloss," I corrected him. "Strawberry champagne number seven."

"And your eyebrows are all . . . pointy and skinny. Like you set them on fire in science lab."

"They're *plucked*," I said indignantly. "Or maybe tweezed. I don't remember what it's called. The point is, it's fashionable."

"If you say so." He wouldn't stop gaping at me. "And why are you making that face?"

"What face?"

"I don't know, you're just . . . you're smiling. Like, really big."

"What's weird about that? I'm not allowed to smile?"

"You just don't usually smile this *much*," Fish said. "It's not like you."

He was saying exactly what I'd been think-ing — but for some reason, I didn't like hearing it come out of his mouth. Max told me I looked *good* with my new makeup and my new attitude. And maybe she was right. After all, she was the one who had done all the research. Who was Fish to tell me that I didn't look like myself? Who was Fish to decide who *I* was supposed to be?

"I bet you don't tell *Brianna* she looks weird in her makeup," I said accusingly.

"That's different. It looks normal on her. But you just look like you're trying to be someone else."

"What do you —" I stopped myself. *Be nice*, I thought, reminding myself what Max had told me to do. *Smile, even when you're not happy. Act like everything's all good, all the time.*

I smiled brighter. "What an *interesting* opinion, Fish. I don't quite agree with it, but I'm always just *thrilled* to hear what you think."

"Stop talking like that! You're weirding me out."

"Stop what, Fish?" I asked, oozing sweetness. "I'd be happy to stop whatever you'd like."

Fish shook his head. "This isn't you. Do you think you're going to win the election by being all fake like this?"

"Why are you so sure it's fake?" I asked, dropping the smile. "Is Brianna the only one who's allowed to be sweet and perky?"

"Brianna's being *herself*," Fish argued. "You're being . . . I don't know what you're being, but I don't like it."

I couldn't believe he was sticking up for Brianna again. Fish was supposed to be *my* best friend. So why was he always on her side? It was like as far as Fish was concerned, Brianna could do no wrong — and I couldn't do anything but.

"You don't like me smiling, but you're totally okay with Brianna insulting your best friends?" I asked.

"She *never* insults you," Fish said. "You're the one who's always saying mean things about her!"

"Oh yeah? What about at Cosmo's the other day? She totally laughed in my face about the election. She said I had no chance."

"She did not. That was Britney and Ashton, and yeah, they're . . ." He shook his head. "I don't know why she hangs out with them, but she's not like that. She's different."

"You're the one who's different," I snapped.

"What's that supposed to mean?"

"Ever since you started hanging around with her, you're just . . . ." I didn't know how to say it. But deep down inside, I knew it was true. "Everything's different."

Fish's eyes widened. "I can't believe you're standing here with all that gunk on your face, and those glittery things in your hair, telling me that *I've* changed. Why are you doing all this stuff, anyway? You didn't even want to be president, and now it's like you'll do anything to win."

"Maybe I just think I'd do a better job." And maybe I thought that if I won, Fish would finally see Brianna for who she really was. Not that I'd ever admit that out loud. *Especially* not to him.

"Oh yeah? Why?"

I stared at him. "I can't believe you even have to ask that."

Fish scooped up his notebook and stuffed it into his backpack. "I've gotta go," he said. "I forgot that I promised my sister I'd help her study for her spelling test tomorrow. Can we do this extra-credit thing another time?"

"Yeah," I grunted. "Whatever. Another time."

He was gone before I realized that we'd just had our first real fight. I wasn't even sure what we were fighting about. After all, I didn't want to argue with him. I just wanted him to tell me that he'd been totally wrong about Brianna Blake and that he was completely, totally, 100 percent on my side — like a best friend should be.

It's like Max said: If you're not with us, you're against us.

Gerald P. Pinchon's rule number one.

☆ CHAPTER SEVEN ☆

"Lip gloss?" Max asked.

I nodded. "Check."

"Eye shadow?"

"Check."

"Mascara?"

"Max, for the last time, I'm wearing all the goop you told me to!" I said, exasperated. "Are you sure I don't look like a clown?"

"For the last time, you don't look like a clown. You look like a president."

"*Candidate* for president," I reminded her.

"That's just a technicality," she said. "It's only a matter of time. Now, are you ready for your close-up?"

I took a deep breath. "I think so."

I didn't know why I was so nervous. It was just an interview on our school's boring TV-news show. A bunch of kids in the journalism club put out an episode every two weeks, and the rest of us have to watch it in social studies class. I'll admit: It's better than listening to a lecture on the Boston Tea Party.

But not much.

"Here," Max said, handing me a sheet of paper.

"What's this?"

"A list of things I think you should try to bring up in the interview."

I sighed with relief. Max thought of everything. I'd spent so much time worrying about my new, "improved" hair and makeup that I hadn't even thought about what I was supposed to say.

"Wait a sec." I took a closer look at the list. "Brianna sleeps with her eyes taped open so her forehead won't get all wrinkly?" I read. "Brianna would have failed math last year, but her father bribed the teacher into giving her an A?" I looked up at Max. "What's all this?"

"Just a few facts about Brianna Blake that I think the voters should know," Max said. She pointed toward number nine on the list. "That one's my favorite."

"When Brianna was a little kid, her mother had

to pay other mothers to bring their kids over for play dates?" I gaped at Max. "Is that *true*?"

Max rocked back and forth from one foot to the other. "Well, it *could* be true. I mean, I think I heard someone saying something like that . . . once."

I shoved the list into her hands. "I'm not going on TV to bash Brianna with a bunch of lies!"

"They're not lies," Max said. "They're just rumors. And Gerald P. Pinchon says that every rumor comes from a kernel of truth. Isn't that what you said you wanted to do? Tell the truth?"

"Even if they were a hundred percent true, it wouldn't matter," I told her. "It's mean, and I'm not doing it."

"*Everyone* does it," Max argued. "According to Gerald P. Pinchon, it's called mudslinging. It's how you win an election. It's not personal."

"It *feels* personal. What if Brianna got up there and told everyone a bunch of lies about me?"

"She probably will," Max said matter-of-factly. "That's why you should strike first." She folded up the paper and slipped it into my pocket. "You don't have to decide now. Just think about it."

But I didn't have to. I already knew what I had to do.

* * *

WSBA *News* was lame. I got that. Look up *lame* in the dictionary, and you would find a picture of the WSBA news desk. Even Sherry Winters, the eighth grade anchor of WSBA *News*, knew it was lame. She was only doing it to get extra credit.

Lame, lame, lame, I told myself, fidgeting in the folding chair, waiting for the interview to start. But then the little red light on the camera flashed on. The director shouted, "Action!" and suddenly, I was in the spotlight. I was going to be on TV. I was going to be a little bit famous. And it didn't feel lame at all.

It felt good.

"So, Callie," Sherry Winters began, "everyone wants to know about you and your surprise run for seventh grade class president. Why don't you tell us a little about yourself, and how you feel about good old Susan B. Anthony Middle School?"

It was just the chance I'd been waiting for.

This was my moment. I could tell the whole school exactly what I thought about things. I could give them a list of everything I thought was wrong with the place. Everything I abhored about it, from A to Z, starting with the way the hall monitors treated us like animals and ending with the way the cafeteria smelled like a zoo. "I think there are a lot of changes we can make around here. For one thing, why aren't we ever allowed to go anywhere without a pass? It's like we're prisoners, and they have to track our every move. Can't we be trusted to —"

That's when I looked up and noticed the camera. Really *noticed* it. I stared at the lens, wondering how many people would be watching this. Did they plan to vote for me?

Would any of them still want to after they heard what I had to say?

Be positive, I heard Max's voice echo in my ears. *Smile.*

People want a president who's sunny and cheerful.

Do you want to win?

I smiled.

"What were you saying?" Sherry Winters asked. I realized I'd totally zoned out.

"Um . . ." *Accentuate the positive*, I told myself. *Talk about what's right.* "I just meant that no one needs to treat us like we're trapped here. Because we're not. We *want* to be here. It's an awesome school, right? And I want to do everything I can to make it even more awesome." I beamed at the camera. "I just want to make a difference."

Sherry Winters looked at me like I'd sprouted wings and antennae.

"Ooookay," she said finally. "Maybe we should move on to the election. Why should people vote for you, and not Brianna?"

"Well, Brianna . . ." I could feel Max's list burning a hole in my pocket, and I realized I didn't even need it. I could think of plenty of reasons not to vote for Brianna, and they were all true. She was spoiled, she was stuck-up, she was superficial — those were just the *S*'s. For years, I had been whining that no one understood what Brianna was *really* like, beneath that pretty, perky mask. This was my chance to tell everyone the truth.

And that was why I'd run for president in the first place, right?

"Well, the thing about Brianna is that she . . ."

But I couldn't do it.

And it wasn't because I was wrong about her. I was right, I knew it. Brianna Blake was evil.

But *I* didn't want to be.

"The thing about Brianna is that she and I are really, um, different people," I said, beaming at the camera. "But we have one thing in common: We both love this school!"

We watched the interview that morning in social studies class.

Of course, when I say "we," I don't actually mean "me." I couldn't stand to look at it. There I was on screen, a real live TV star. Except that it wasn't me. It was some girl in strawberry lip gloss who couldn't stop smiling. It was a perky, cheery girl talking about *awesome* dances and *awesome* fund-raisers and all the other *awesome* things she would do if she got to be the *awesome* president of the *awesome* class council.

I was a total fraud. Everyone would notice.

But they didn't.

They clapped.

"Love your hair!" Bethany Allen called from the other side of the room. She waved her black headband in the air.

"Totally cute shirt!" Mia Phillips added. Maybe she'd forgotten that she was wearing a pink armband.

"Yeah, and you sound totally, uh, presidential," Jackson Cummings said. I knew Max was still feeding him brownies to be nice to me, but he almost sounded like he meant it.

Even Mr. Hamilton (decked out in a black Smashing Pumpkins T-shirt that scored a seven point five) looked surprised. "Very telegenic," he said, nodding. "This election may make a real

115

politician out of you yet." The way he said it, I wasn't quite sure he meant it as a good thing. But then he whipped out his crooked grin. "I hope you'll remember us all when you're powerful and famous."

"I'll always remember the little people," I shot back, smiling.

Mr. Hamilton chuckled, which made me glow. He was always making us laugh, but it wasn't easy to get him to join in. "I just hope you can fit that big head through the doorway on your way out of the classroom."

The words popped out of my mouth before I knew what I was saying. "When I'm president, I guess I'll just have to build bigger doors."

The class burst into laughter.

That happened a lot when I spoke up in class. But it wasn't usually because I meant to. Laughing *at* me? That was old news. But laughing *with* me? That was different.

That was *good*.

"Maybe you were right not to spread those rumors," Max whispered as the class calmed down and Mr. Hamilton began introducing the next segment of the tape — Brianna's interview.

"So you're saying you were *wrong*?" I raised my eyebrows and grinned.

"Not wrong, necessarily, but it was better your way. You sounded friendly, positive, happy — all the things anyone could want in a president."

"You don't think I seemed kind of . . . fake?" I whispered back. I couldn't believe that even *Max* had been fooled. Didn't she see that I was pretending to be someone I wasn't? Someone cheerful and shallow?

Someone like Brianna Blake.

"You were perfect," Max assured me.

But she didn't really answer my question.

I wished I could ask Fish what *he* thought. But we hadn't really talked since our fight the other night. And he didn't turn around to look at me after the interview. He just stared at the TV screen, waiting for Brianna's interview to come on.

She looked perfect, of course. Beautiful and polished and smooth, like she was born to be on TV. And all of her answers were perfect, too. Just like me, she said all this stuff about how she loved the school and wanted to help everyone have a "super-fun year!" But when she said it, she sounded like she actually believed it. I couldn't figure out how she did that.

"Callie?" she chirped, when Sherry Winters asked her about the competition.

I straightened up in my chair, nervous (but also a little excited) to hear what she would say.

Brianna giggled softly. "It's so much fun to have someone to run against," she said, smiling. "And Callie's such a sweet, adorable girl."

In front of me, Fish snorted. Max choked back a laugh. I couldn't blame them.

Sweet?

Adorable?

Was she talking about a different Callie Singer?

"For example, I just happened to come across this picture of her from when she was little," Brianna went on, smiling sweetly at Sherry Winters. "Isn't she just adorable?" She held up a photo. "Can the camera get close enough to see this?"

I gasped.

I slid down in my seat.

I wanted to slide all the way under the desk. Under the *floor*.

I wanted to disappear.

The class's laughter roared in my ears. These were the kind of laughs I was used to. I just wasn't used to it hurting this much. Not that I blamed them. You'd laugh, too, if you saw it. Me at five years old, dressed up like cupid for my parents' stupid Valentine's Day party, wearing pink tights, a pink leotard, white wings, and a giant white *diaper.*

Only two other people in the world had a copy of that picture. Two people who had found it in one of my mom's photo albums and begged and pleaded for copies of their very own. Two people who had *promised* never to show it to anyone, never ever in a million years, no matter what. Two people.

Number one: Max.

Number two . . .

My eyes were lasers in the back of his neck.

He wasn't laughing. But he didn't turn around, either. Probably because he couldn't face me.

He couldn't face what he'd done to me, his best friend.

Former best friend.

"How could you?" I shouted as soon as we hit the hallway.

"What?" Fish asked, pretending to be clueless. I wasn't buying it.

Max dragged us down the hall, away from the crowd. I knew she didn't want the potential voters to see the real me, the angry me.

But what did I care which me they saw? What difference did it make, now that they'd seen me in a *diaper*?

"How could you give her that picture?" I could feel the tears threatening to spurt out of my eyes, like they always do when I'm mad. I blinked hard.

"I didn't!" Fish protested. "How could you think I would do that to you?"

"If not you, then who?" I asked. "The only people who have copies of that picture are you, me, and Max."

"So it *had* to be you," Max added quickly. "Do you really want Brianna to win the election that much?"

"I don't care *who* wins the stupid election!" Fish retorted. "Since when do I lie to you?"

"I guess since you and Brianna turned into BFFs," I snapped. "I don't even *know* you anymore."

Fish laughed, but it wasn't a happy sound. "Are you kidding me?" he asked. "*You* don't know *me*?" He rolled his eyes. "Did you even *hear* yourself in that interview? How fake can you get? You're calling me a liar? Every word out of your mouth was a lie!"

"It's not the same!" I protested.

"You're right, it's worse!" he exclaimed. "Because I'm not lying at all. You two are going crazy over this dumb election — and you're ruining everything."

The tears were coming whether I wanted them or not. I turned my back on Fish, so he wouldn't see. "You're the one who ruined everything," I muttered. "How am I supposed to forgive you for this?"

"Who's asking you to?" Fish snapped.

I heard him stomp away down the hall. When I turned around, he was gone.

Max put her hand on my arm. "It's okay," she said. "He'll be back."

I shrugged her off. "It's *not* okay! How could he do that to me?"

Max bit her lip. "Well, maybe he's not lying."

I barely heard her. "It wasn't all his fault, though," I said. "He would never have done it, if it wasn't for *her*. Brianna's got some kind of evil hold on him."

For the first time, I knew why my mother never wanted me to use the word *hate*. She was right. It was a powerful word. It wasn't the same as *detest*, *despise*, *loathe*, or even *abhor*. It was too big and too powerful to hold inside.

I *hated* Brianna Blake.

And I was going to do something about it.

Max had a dentist appointment after school, but she promised me that when she got home, we would figure out how to handle Diapergate.

I couldn't wait that long.

I'm sure Max would have come up with some kind of subtle, devious, brilliant plot to get back at Brianna. After all, she had Gerald P. Pinchon on her side.

All I had was my anger — and my black permanent marker.

So that day, I hung around school until everyone else was gone. I waited until the halls were empty and dark. Then I waited one more hour, just to be sure. I didn't think about what I was about to do. I just thought about how Fish had betrayed me, and how Brianna had made him, and how the whole school was laughing at me and calling me "Diaper Girl" behind my back.

And then I crept through the halls. I uncapped my marker. And I hurried over to the first "Vote for Brianna!" poster I could find. It was one of the beautiful ones that Fish had drawn himself, with a big picture of Brianna's big head.

I hesitated.

What am I doing? I thought, gripping the uncapped marker. *This isn't me.*

But then:

Remember Diaper Girl, I told myself, shuddering. *That shouldn't be me, either. But it is, thanks to Brianna.*

I drew a thick, black X across her grinning face. And that felt so good, I drew another.

On the next poster, I gave her a mustache and a beard.

On the third, I drew a speech bubble dribbling out of her mouth that read: THINKING IS HARD WORK. I added an empty thought bubble puffing out of her head.

And then, all alone in the dark hallway, surrounded by wall after wall of posters I'd ruined, I laughed.

Hours later, I still heard that laugh.

I heard it while I was lying in bed, trying to fall asleep. It sounded like the laugh of someone cruel, someone spiteful.

It didn't sound like me . . . but I knew it was.

I had felt so good, standing there in the hallway with my black permanent marker. I'd felt like I was doing the right thing. I was getting the revenge I deserved. But that night, I just felt sick.

Brianna made me do it, I told myself. But I knew that wasn't true.

I'd done it myself. I couldn't blame Max for putting the idea in my head, I couldn't blame Fish for selling me out. I couldn't even blame Brianna for throwing the first fistful of mud.

I could only blame me.

I wanted to sneak out of the house, run back to school, and erase everything I'd drawn. But I couldn't take it back. I could only lie there and think about what I'd done. I kept trying to fool myself into believing it was the right thing. But I knew the truth, deep down, where it really hurt.

It was wrong.

☆ CHAPTER EIGHT ☆

I woke up the next morning still feeling sick. But not sick enough to stay home from school. At least, not according to my mom. I tried to argue that I needed to stay home to preserve my mental health. She didn't buy it. Then I tried staging a sit-in. I refused to leave the kitchen — right up to the moment she started telling me about the day I was born. In detail. Gross, gross detail.

I was out of there in thirty seconds.

Lucky for me, I'd waited so long I'd missed the bus. Lucky because *Fish* was on the bus. And there was no way I was going to face him until I absolutely had to.

"You know, if it was up to me, you'd be walking," my brother said from the driver's seat of our mom's Pontiac. He switched the radio to a heavy metal station he knew I hated. "I should stop the car and kick you out right here."

"I dare you," I told him. "Then *you'd* get to explain it to Mom at dinner tonight."

I was half-hoping that he would throw me out. At least it would give me a good excuse not to go to school. But he kept driving. Hobbes may have had his license, but didn't have his own car. Which meant following Mom's instructions. Even when they were instructions we both despised.

"Whatever. Just don't think I'm giving you a ride home."

"You're such a loving brother," I told him, sticking out my tongue. "How'd I get so lucky?"

He grunted. "Just jump out quick when I stop. I don't want anyone I know to see me with you."

"Am I really that embarrassing?" I was joking. Mostly.

"At least you're not wearing any more of that goop on your face. That's an improvement."

I'd stuffed all of my new makeup under the sink. What was the point of pretending I was perky and perfect after what I'd done to Brianna's posters? Once everyone found out the truth . . .

Let's just say it wouldn't matter how presidential I looked. Not if I was no longer running for president.

Still, I couldn't admit any of that to my oaf of a brother. "Some of us *care* about how we look," I informed Hobbes. It actually felt kind of good to be trading insults with him. As long as I was still in the car with him, everything was normal. It was only outside that my life was spinning out of control.

"Oh, I care about how you look." Hobbes stuck his finger down his throat and made a retching noise. "You know how hard it is to eat dinner every night while I'm looking at your face?"

"You know how hard it is to breathe when I'm smelling your stink?"

He slammed his foot down on the brake and screeched to a stop in front of the school. "Out."

I didn't move.

Hobbes lifted his arm and lurched toward me, his armpit leading the way. "You want some more of that stink?"

I got out of the car even faster than I'd gotten out of the house.

By the time I got into school, the janitors and the teachers were already pulling all of Brianna's posters down — and mine, too, just to be fair. But they didn't do it quickly enough. The whole school was talking about the ruined posters, wondering who could have done it.

Brianna's face was pale. Britney and Ashton

swept her through the halls like bodyguards. They shot hostile glances at the rest of us, like they were expecting someone to attack. At least Fish wasn't with them.

It doesn't matter where Fish is or who he hangs out with, I reminded myself. *You're done with him. Just like he's obviously done with you.*

Max caught up with me at my locker.

"Was it you?" she whispered.

I stared at my sneakers and let my hair fall in front of my eyes, so that I didn't have to look at her.

"Everyone's saying it had to be you," she said. "But I know you'd never do something like that. Me? Maybe. But you? No way."

I shrugged. I didn't want to lie to her. But I couldn't force myself to tell the truth.

"We should probably meet to discuss strategy," Max said. She was already flipping through her clipboard, like she hadn't noticed that I wasn't answering her questions. "This could work in our favor, if we spin it right —"

"Was it you?" Fish asked from behind me. Unlike Max, he didn't sound curious or impressed. He just sounded angry. "Did you two ruin my posters?"

"I didn't have anything to do with it!" Max snapped.

I didn't say anything.

"And besides," Max continued. "They were *Brianna's* posters, not yours."

"I drew them," Fish said. "They were *my* art. And now they're in the trash."

"I . . ." I stopped. There was a big lump at the base of my throat. I couldn't squeeze any words out around it. I could barely even swallow. "I, um . . ."

And then a hand clamped down on my shoulder, saving me.

Sort of.

"Ms. Singer, the principal would like to see you in his office," the hall monitor said in her deep, gurgly voice. *"Now."*

"I know it was you," Brianna said. Her voice was like steel, cold and hard.

We were sitting in the narrow hallway outside the principal's office, waiting for him to call us inside.

"You don't have to lie to me," she said. "I'm not going to tell on you. But I know it was you."

I wasn't going to admit anything. I had decided I would confess to the principal. But not to Brianna. No matter how horrible I felt, I still couldn't do that.

She sighed. "I guess I deserved it. For that diaper picture. Fair's fair, right?"

I jerked my head up and looked at her in surprise. She was actually smiling. And not the fake, pretty, perky, "Aren't-I-beautiful" Brianna Blake smile — a real one. It was sort of crooked, but it went all the way to her eyes.

"I didn't want to do it," she continued, "but Britney and Ashton were totally obsessed, they wouldn't stop bothering me about it. Finally, I just gave in to get them to stop talking, you know?" she shook her head. "Sorry, I guess."

I couldn't believe it. Brianna was apologizing to *me*?

"Yeah, well . . . I'm sorry, too, I guess," I told her, hoping I wouldn't have to actually *say* what I was sorry for.

Brianna sighed and leaned her head back against the wall. "I just wish this whole election thing was over, you know? Like I could just fast-forward and skip right to the good part."

"The good part?" I asked. I figured she was planning some big victory party. That was just like Brianna Blake, already certain she would win.

"You know, class council meetings, planning the dances, meeting with the teachers."

I couldn't believe she was actually excited about

that stuff. The idea of sitting through a class council meeting, listening to people blab about dance decorations, kind of made me want to puke.

"I've got all these new ideas for the class fundraiser this year," Brianna chirped. "I was thinking about it over the summer, and I really think that we should — oh." She stopped and gave herself a little shake. "Well, I guess I'm not supposed to be sharing secrets with the enemy." She laughed. "That's what Britney and Ashton are always saying. Silly, right?"

"Um, right," I said weakly.

"I mean, I figure when this election is over, we'll all be on the same side again. It's just like you said in your interview — it's about making the school a better place, right?"

"Uh-huh," I said, nodding.

I couldn't believe it. Was she *serious*? Did she actually want to win this election so that she could *help* people? I had always assumed Brianna was a total fake, just smiling and being nice to people because she knew it would make her popular. And popularity meant power.

But if she was sincere, if she was just acting friendly and cheerful because she really *was* friendly and cheerful, that meant there was only one giant fake sitting in that hallway.

And it wasn't Brianna Blake.

"The principal will see you now," Mr. McCourt's secretary said, poking her head out into the hallway. We trooped into the office and sat down in front of his wide wooden desk.

"Girls, I'm *very* disappointed with the way this presidential campaign is unfolding," Mr. McCourt told us sternly. I had never been called into the principal's office before. In fact, I had never really seen Mr. McCourt close up. I hadn't noticed before that there was gray hair growing out of his ears, or that all the nails on his left hand were covered with Band-Aids. I wondered if he was trying to stop biting his nails. Max did the same thing for a few months in sixth grade. It didn't work.

"Whoever damaged those posters" — Mr. McCourt stared hard at me — "has done Brianna a very serious wrong. Brianna, I'm not entirely sure that displaying that photograph of Callie was in keeping with the spirit of Susan B. Anthony Middle School, either. But the vandalism of the campaign posters is another matter altogether. Things are getting out of control with this campaign. I've spoken with Mr. Hamilton about the possibility of canceling the election before things go too far."

"You can't!" Brianna blurted out.

"I'm afraid I can," Mr. McCourt said. "I can and, if necessary, I will. Now, Callie, is there anything you'd like to say to me about the incident that took place here last night?"

This was it. I was going to tell him everything. I would confess my crime and offer to drop out of the race. And then I would beg him not to expel me.

"Mr. McCourt, I . . ." My voice was shaking. But I had to get it out. "I have to tell you that —"

"That she's been very upset by everyone assuming that she's behind the vandalism," Brianna said quickly, shooting me a look that said *Stop talking NOW*. "I know Callie, and she'd never do such a thing." She flashed Mr. McCourt a brilliant smile. "And while I was extremely hurt by whoever destroyed those posters, I certainly don't think it's fair to *either* of us for you to cancel the election. In fact, it's not fair to the school, Mr. McCourt. What about the voice of the people? What about the democratic process? Shouldn't the student body be allowed to have their say?" Her eyes glistened with fake tears. I had to admit it, she was good.

Really good.

"Well . . ." Mr. McCourt cleared his throat, surprised by Brianna's passionate speech. "If both of you girls promise to remain on your best, most civil behavior . . ."

"We do!" Brianna said eagerly. I just nodded, afraid that if I opened my mouth to say anything, the truth would pop out. Whether I wanted it to or not.

"Then why don't you shake hands, and let's have a good, clean election!"

We shook hands. And when Mr. McCourt turned his head away for a second, Brianna winked. Without thinking, I winked back. It was almost like we were on the same side.

"Thanks," I said, once we were safely out of the office and on our way back to class. And I meant it. "You didn't have to, back there, you know. Cover for me."

"I didn't do it for you," she said. "Mr. McCourt can't cancel this election."

"But if he knew the truth, then you'd probably get to be president automatically," I pointed out.

She shook her head. "Then it wouldn't be official. It wouldn't really count. It'd be okay if this was last year, when nobody ran against me. But now it's different. This year, if I win against you, it'll be because people vote for me. Because they *choose* me. You know what I mean?"

"I guess," I said, even though I wasn't sure I did. Winning was winning, right? "Well, I should probably head to math . . ."

"Hey, before you go —" Brianna had a weird look on her face, one I'd never seen before. Then I realized: She looked unsure of herself. "You should give Jacob a break, okay?"

"Who's — oh, right. Fish. That's really none of your —" I stopped. I was going to tell her it was none of her business how I treated Fish, since he was *my* best friend, not hers. But I couldn't say something like that. Not after what she'd just done. "It's just . . . it's complicated," I said instead.

"He didn't give me that picture," she said. "He wouldn't do that to you."

"Then who did?" I asked. "Only three people have a copy of that picture, and if it wasn't Fish —"

"I can't say who," Brianna said quickly. "I promised. But it wasn't Fish. So if there really are only three people with a copy, you'll figure it out. If you want to."

"Okay. Fine. Whatever. I have to go," I said. I didn't want to think about what she meant. Not that it wasn't obvious. We learned the process of elimination back in third grade, right between estimating and why you shouldn't feed the class goldfish pieces of a Snickers bar. (At least Goldie got a nice funeral before we flushed her.) I knew how it worked. I knew that if I didn't give Brianna the picture, and Fish didn't give Brianna the picture . . .

That's where I stopped myself. I just needed my life to go back to normal, and my friends to be my friends again. *All* of my friends. "Uh, good luck with the rest of the campaign and everything."

"You too," Brianna said. "Not that you need it."

"What do you mean?" I asked.

"Don't you know?" she said. The smile was back. But now that I'd seen her real smile, I could tell that this one was fake, like the one you give your best friend when she accidentally hits you in the face with a soccer ball and you want her to think it doesn't hurt. (Just so you know: It did. A *lot*.) "Everyone wants to vote for you. I've been president forever." She shrugged. "I guess they think it's time for a change. Maybe they're right. I just . . ." The smile crumbled a little around the edges. "I really want to be president, you know? Well, of course you know. You want it, too."

Did I want to be president? I wanted to win, I knew that.

But was it the same thing?

"The election's not until Monday," I pointed out. "Anything could happen."

"Yeah," she said. And suddenly I noticed that her eyes were glistening again. But this time, it didn't seem so fake. "I guess anything could."

"Oh, come on," Max said on the phone that night. "She was playing you."

"I don't think so," I told her. "You should have seen it. She was really into the whole class council thing. The fund-raiser, the dance, all that, I think she *really* wants to win."

"Well, so do we," Max said.

"No, not like that." I kicked off my shoes and bounced onto my bed, staring up at the multicolored ceiling. Last summer, Fish had climbed up to the very top rung of the ladder and spattered it with all my favorite colors of paint. It took him a week, and he wouldn't let me help — he said it was an early birthday present.

But my birthday's in December.

"We want to *win*," I said. Max knew that by *win* I meant *beat Brianna*. "But she actually wants to *be* president."

"I don't see the difference. But anyway —"

"She said something else, too," I added quietly.

Part of me really didn't want to know the truth. But another part of me had to ask. "About the photograph. You know, the diaper thing."

"Yes?" Max's voice was even softer than mine.

"She said it didn't come from Fish."

There was a pause.

"Did she say who she got it from?" Max asked.

The tone of her voice told me all I needed to know.

I squeezed the phone tight — because I knew if I didn't, I'd throw it across the room. The words choked in my throat, but I spit them out. "How could you?"

"You're going to believe something *Brianna* said?" Max asked. "She's just trying to ruin your campaign."

"*You're* the one trying to ruin my campaign!" I accused her. "By humiliating me in front of the whole school."

"I —"

I waited for her to deny it.

She sighed. "I did it for you."

"What's that supposed to mean?"

"I was just trying to —"

"No!" I shouted. "You know what? Forget I asked. It doesn't matter why. It just matters that you did it — and then you stood there, and you let me call

Fish a liar, and now he hates me, and I ruined all his posters, and everything's horrible, and it's All! Your! Fault!"

I hung up the phone.

It rang again a second later, but I didn't answer.

"It's for you, *Calliope*!" Hobbes shouted through the door.

"Tell her I'm not here!" I called back. "Tell her I'll never be here."

"She's popping an enormous zit in the center of her forehead," I heard him say into the phone. "She'll call you back once she washes off all the pus."

Under normal circumstances, I would have killed him. But it got the job done — the phone didn't ring again.

I crawled into bed and pulled the covers over my face. I wanted to block out the world. *Two weeks ago, I had two best friends,* I thought.

So how did I end up all alone?

☆ CHAPTER NINE ☆

When I was eight years old, my dad got invited to speak at a conference in Florida and decided we should all drive down with him. After all, what could be more fun than a family road trip? Oh, I don't know, maybe:

A dentist appointment.

A standardized test.

Gym class.

All on the same day.

First of all, the conference was in Florida. A state that is, incidentally, about a thousand miles away from our house in New Jersey. But wait, it gets better. My dad thought it would be *extra* fun to make the whole drive without stopping. I mean, we stopped for bathroom breaks, and to pick up rubbery fast-food burgers every few hours, but that was it. Hour after hour after hour. After hour. Trapped in the car. With my parents. And my brother, who, after the first twelve hours, started to smell.

My left foot fell asleep somewhere around Maryland. By Virginia, I couldn't turn my neck to the left. In South Carolina, my brother spilled his soda in my lap. I was soggy right through Georgia.

For a long time, I was pretty sure it was the worst weekend I would ever have in my life.

But the weekend before the election was worse.

I spent most of it in bed, trying to figure out where everything had gone wrong. I told my parents I was sick, but that was a lie. I just couldn't make myself get up, get dressed, and pretend everything was normal. Everything was so *not* normal.

Fish wasn't speaking to me. I wasn't speaking to Max.

And on Monday I was supposed to go to school like nothing was wrong, march up onstage, and tell the whole school why they should vote for me.

Why would they vote for me? How could I run the school? I couldn't even run my own life.

My computer dinged with another IM. I knew it was Max. Again. She'd been IMing me all weekend.

I'd just ignored her. But lying in bed for two days can get kind of boring. No matter how mad I was — and I was plenty mad — at least reading her message would give me something to do.

I got out of bed and went over to the computer. Then I gasped.

The message wasn't from Max. It was from Fish.

I'm sorry. We need 2 talk. Meet me @ Pinocchio's 2nite @8?

Pinocchio's was *our* place, where Max, Fish, and I always went after school for greasy pizza and flat soda. The food was terrible, but we loved it, anyway. For us, it was like home.

Emphasis on *was*. We hadn't been there since the beginning of the campaign. And I'd begun to think we might never go there again.

But if Fish wanted to talk . . . *Maybe he wants to apologize for teaming up with Brianna,* I thought. Maybe he was finally ready to admit he was wrong. And if he was, I could apologize, too. I'd been wrong to call him a liar, and to think he could betray me like that. I *wanted* to say I was sorry.

I just didn't want to say it first.

*   *   *

When I got to Pinocchio's, Fish was already half-way through a slice of anchovy pizza. I pulled up a chair.

Silence.

"So?" he finally asked.

"So," I said.

More silence.

"I'm waiting," he said.

"Waiting for what?"

He tore off a piece of crust and popped it in his mouth. But he didn't offer me any, even though I know he doesn't like the crust — and *he* knows I think it's the best part. "You said you wanted to talk. So talk."

I thought I must have heard him wrong.

"*Me?* You said *you* wanted to talk. Aren't you going to apologize?"

"Apologize?" He looked at me like I was speaking a foreign language. "Apologize for what?"

"You're the one who dragged me down here," I snapped. "Why don't *you* tell *me*?"

"*You're* the one who wanted to meet *me* here," Fish said. He pushed his chair away from the table and stood up. "I thought you actually had something important to say, but apparently —"

"Wait!" The voice came from the back of the restaurant. And a moment later, Max appeared.

143

"Don't go," she said. Or maybe she begged. "Please. Stay."

Fish sat down again.

I wanted to ask Max what she thought she was doing, suckering us into showing up, but I wasn't speaking to her. That made asking questions kind of tricky. So I just folded my arms and glared down at the table.

"You won't answer your phone, and you won't IM me back," Max told me. "I had to talk to you. I had to say I'm sorry. And even if you're going to hate me forever, I *know* you want to make up with Fish. So I thought maybe, if I could help . . ."

"What's she talking about?" Fish asked, frowning.

"She's the one who gave the picture to Brianna," I muttered. "I know it wasn't you."

"You're kidding me!" Fish exclaimed. "But why would —"

"It was stupid," Max said quickly. "I know that. I knew that as soon as I did it. It's just that Callie was feeling so guilty about fighting back, and I knew that if we were going to win this election, she *had* to fight." She turned to me. "So I thought, maybe if you were getting revenge on Brianna, if you *knew* she was the enemy . . ."

144

"But why did *I* have to be the enemy, too?" Fish asked.

"Because according to Gerald P. Pinchon —" Max stopped herself and shook her head. "No. It's not his fault. It's me. I thought that if you were on Brianna's side, that meant you had to be against us. And I talked Callie into thinking it, too. I messed everything up."

"No," I said quietly. I turned to Fish. I hated to admit that I was wrong . . . but I also hated having him mad at me. "I shouldn't have been so angry that you were working for Brianna," I admitted. "I shouldn't have been so, um . . ." I covered my mouth behind my hands, ". . . jealous."

"What was that?" he asked, cupping a hand to his ear.

"Jealous!" I repeated louder. "Okay? I was jealous! She's got everyone in the whole school on her side, and I just have the two of you, and you're *my* friend, and she was trying to steal you away, and it wasn't fair!" The words spilled out before I could stop them.

Fish gave me a weird look. It was almost . . . a smile?

"Are you nuts?" he asked. "No one can 'steal me.' It's not like I'm your wallet or something. I'm your best friend. No matter how much I help out

Brianna, or even if I *am* her friend, I'm still *your* best friend."

"You are?" I asked. I felt the way you do after finally getting over the flu, when it seems amazing that you can take a deep breath without choking. "Still? Even after all the things I said to you?"

"Still," he nodded. "And I said some things, too, I guess. I shouldn't have gone on and on about you being fake. I know you're just doing what you have to do."

"I don't *have* to do anything," I admitted. "I was doing what I thought I *should* do. I was just . . ."

"Wrong?" Fish suggested, grinning.

I sagged in the chair. "Maybe. Yeah."

He dangled the last piece of pizza crust in my face. "Any chance this would make you feel better?"

I snatched it out of his hand and popped it in my mouth. And just like that, things were back to normal again. Well, except for . . .

"Um, guys?" Max said, clearing her throat. "I'm still here and still, you know, a horrible, horrible friend that desperately needs your forgiveness?"

Fish and I exchanged a glance. "What do you think?" he asked.

I bit down on the corners of my lips, holding back a smile. "I don't know," I said, torturing Max just a little. "She did turn me into Diaper Girl in front of the whole school."

"I thought that diaper was a pretty good look for you. Really brought out your eyes," Fish teased. "Hey, you still have it? Maybe you should wear it for your big speech tomorrow."

"If I had a slice of pizza, I'd cram it in your face," I warned him. "And Max." I turned back to her. "I should smash a *whole* pizza in your face. But since we didn't order one . . ." I grinned. "I guess you're forgiven."

She let out a sigh of relief that sounded like a deflating balloon. Then she collapsed into a chair next to us. "We're good?" she asked. "Really?"

"Really," I assured her. "Just promise me you'll never do anything like that again. And we're tearing that picture to shreds. *Every* copy."

"I still don't get why you went so crazy," Fish said, raising his eyebrows at Max.

Max sighed. "Do you want the truth?"

"Yes!" Fish and I both yelled. It was about time.

"I guess the real reason I wanted you to win so badly is that I kind of wish . . ." Max cleared her throat. Her cheeks turned tomato-red. That almost never happened to Max. "I wish that I was the one running. You know, that *I* could be president."

Fish and I both looked at her in shock. *"You?"* we asked.

"Hey, it's not *so* crazy!" she protested.

"It's not crazy at all," I said quickly. "I just don't get it. If you wanted to run, why didn't you? Why nominate *me*?"

"Well, for one thing, I know how you feel about all that stuff — class council, planning dances, all that rah-rah school-spirit stuff. You think it's totally lame."

"Well . . . yeah," I admitted. "But so what?"

"I didn't want you to think *I* was lame, too," she said.

I rolled my eyes. "You *are* totally lame. But only for worrying about that."

"Yeah, I guess I know that," she admitted. "I told myself that you were the reason I didn't run. But the real reason is . . . I knew I could never win."

"What? Why not?" Fish asked. "I mean, look at you, you're a political genius! You turned Callie's campaign into a total monster. And I mean that only *sort of* in a bad way."

"Sure, I'm great for behind the scenes." Max stared down at her napkin, twisting it into a tight little ball. "When I'm trying to get people to vote for *Callie*. That's easy. But me? I'm an annoying know-it-all control freak."

"Watch it," I cut in. "That's my best friend you're talking about."

"I'm just being realistic," Max said. "No one would want me in charge of anything. No one would vote for me."

I balled up my napkin, too, and threw it at her forehead. "You really have no idea how great you are, do you?" I asked. "*You're* the one who's all into politics. You're the one who knows everything about this stuff. You *should* be the one running — and you're the only one here who thinks you couldn't win. Right, Fish?"

He shrugged. "President Max? Sounds good to me."

Max tapped a finger on the ridge of her glasses. "It doesn't really matter now," she said. "Callie's the one running, which means Callie's the one with the big speech to give tomorrow. And" — she pulled a piece of paper out of her pocket — "I brought some guidelines for you to —"

"No!" I cried, throwing another napkin at her. "No more Gerald P. Pinchon! No more rules! No more strategizing!"

Max raised her eyebrows. "These rules aren't out of a book," she said. "Gerald P. Pinchon is back in the library, where he belongs. I made these up myself."

"Yourself?" Fish asked, sounding doubtful. "You didn't get them off the Internet?"

Max shook her head.

"Or from the newspaper?" I added.

Max shook her head again.

"Or —"

"I do *occasionally* think of things myself, you know," Max said indignantly. She unfolded the paper. "Rule number one: Be whoever you want to be."

Fish nodded. "Sounds good so far."

"Rule number two," Max continued. "Say whatever you want to say."

"Works for me," I said.

"Rule number three: Tell the truth."

"No more shady promises about stuff I can't deliver?" I asked. "No more fake smiles and plastic cheeriness?"

"No more," Max said firmly.

"Excellent," Fish and I said together.

"And one more rule," Max concluded. "From now on, I, Maxine Samuels, your official campaign manager, will keep my mouth shut."

When I got home that night, I should have felt better. My best friends were my best friends again, and I knew that was all that really mattered. But I couldn't stop thinking about the next day. On Monday morning, I was supposed to give a speech to the whole school, telling them why they should vote for me. And then on Monday afternoon: the election.

I hadn't even started writing my speech yet. Mostly because I had no idea what I was supposed to say.

"Be yourself," Max reminded me, before we left Pinocchio's. But with everything that had happened over the last two weeks, I didn't even know who that was anymore.

I shuffled into the kitchen and slumped down at the table. My mom was sitting across from me, typing something on her laptop with one hand and holding a tofu cookie in the other. My dad was at the stove, cooking up some kind of foul-smelling stew that I knew I'd be stuck eating for the rest of the week. If I survived.

"You okay, hon?" my mom asked, finally looking up from her computer. "You nervous about your big day tomorrow?"

"Not nervous, really," I said. I definitely couldn't tell my parents the whole truth about the campaign, because then I would have to tell them what I did to Brianna's posters. "Just, um, I don't know. I'm supposed to give this speech about why I want to be president, and I guess I don't really know why. I don't even know if I *do* anymore."

My father sat down at the table with us. "Do you want my advice?"

I paused. I never ask my parents for advice, because I know better.

But this was an emergency.

"Sure," I told him.

"Taking on a position of leadership is a big responsibility, not a decision that should be taken lightly. Hobbes tells us —"

I tried to stop him there, but it was no use.

"'It belonged of right to whatsoever man or assembly that hath the sovereignty to be judge both of the means of peace and defense,'" he recited. "Just think about that."

Great.

"You should also remember," my mother added, "the cautionary example of Peisistratus and Cleisthenes, which teaches us that while democracy can arise from the ashes of tyranny, there exists . . ."

I zoned out.

For a *long* time.

"Um, okay," I said, when Mom finally stopped talking. "I should probably get some sleep, you know. Before the big day." Don't get me wrong, I love my parents — sometimes I even *like* them — and I knew they were trying to help. But some things would just be easier if they lived in the real world. "But thanks," I added. "That really helped."

Which was sort of true.

It helped me remember never to ask them for advice again.

Hobbes — my brother, not the one who's been dead for four hundred years — found me curled up under the desk in my room. It's where I used to go when I was little and the whole world seemed out to get me. I would sneak under the desk, draw my knees up to my chest, and wait in the dark until things felt better.

"What's with you, *Calliope*?" Hobbes asked, poking his head into my hiding place.

I should have reminded him that he's not supposed to come into my room without knocking. In fact, he's not supposed to come in at all. But I wasn't in the mood.

"Go away," I said.

"You crying?" he asked, surprised.

Just my luck, the one time my brother decided to pay attention to anything other than his hair and his muscles — and it was the one time I wanted to be absolutely alone.

"No." I sniffled.

"Come on, get out of there." He grabbed my hands and yanked me off the floor, just like he used to do when we were kids. Back before he got too bored and too busy to hang out with me. He spun me around and let go at just the right moment, so I went sailing onto my bed. I landed with a soft thud. And I couldn't help but smile.

"Better," he said. "So, what's up?"

"Nothing," I said. Maybe if I needed help learning a football play or figuring out how much to bench-press, I would ask Hobbes for help. But otherwise? Not a chance.

"Nervous about the election tomorrow?"

I couldn't believe he'd remembered. The surprise must have shown on my face.

"Hey, I pay attention," he protested.

"I'm not nervous," I said. "I just have to write my speech about why I want to be president."

"So?"

"So I don't know the answer."

"Maybe that should tell you something," he said.

I knew I should have kicked him out of my room when I had the chance. "Look, I know you think it's a totally dumb idea that I'm running, and that I'd be a terrible president, and that no one would ever vote for me —"

"Hey!" he cut in. "I never said that. It just doesn't seem like the kind of thing that you're into."

I sighed. "It's not."

Hobbes looked over his shoulder, like he was checking for witnesses. Then he leaned toward me. "If you repeat this to anyone, I'll deny it," he said quietly. "But . . ."

"But what?" I grumbled.

"But I always thought it was kind of cool, the way you only do stuff you really want to do."

I didn't get it.

"You know," he continued. "Everyone else is all about what other people think of them, and whether they're cool or popular or whatever. But you? You just say what you want to say, do what you want to do. You don't care what other people think. At least, you didn't used to."

He was right, I realized. I didn't.

But ever since I'd started this campaign, I'd been doing what other people told me to do. I'd started caring about what they thought of me. And then I'd changed everything — the way I looked, the way I talked, the way I acted — just so they would vote for me.

And I still didn't even know why I wanted to win!

"Thanks, Hobbes," I said, wondering whether aliens had landed and turned my brother into some kind of pod person. It seemed unlikely, since he was acting more like a human being than he had in years. "If you tell anyone I said this, *I'll* deny it, but . . . that actually kind of helps."

"You know what else could help?" he asked.

"What?"

Hobbes grinned. "Putting a paper bag over that ugly monkey face of yours, *Calliope*," he said, and burst out laughing.

"I'd rather look like a monkey than smell like one, loser." But I was laughing, too. Hobbes threw a pillow at me, but I caught it and walloped him in the face. He grabbed me and started twisting my arms into pretzels. But even though he was bigger, I was quicker, and soon I was tickling him, and he was laughing too hard to push me away.

And, if you ever tell anyone I said this, I'll deny it, but . . .

For just a few minutes, I was kind of glad to have a big brother.

☆ CHAPTER TEN ☆

". . . and this year, we're going to hold the biggest, wildest, most successful winter carnival Susan B. Anthony Middle School has ever seen!" Brianna shouted into the microphone. The applause drowned out whatever she said next. It was the third time she'd been interrupted by clapping, and she was only two minutes into her speech.

I tried to pay attention, but I couldn't. I was too nervous. I had my own speech in my lap. I hated it. I'd written it at three A.M., and I was pretty sure it didn't make any sense.

"With me as your president," Brianna continued, "every student will have a voice! And your voice will be heard! I'll work day and night to make sure that our end-of-the-year dance is a spectacular, unforgettable night of fun. It's going to be the best spring dance Susan B. Anthony Middle School has ever seen!"

Cue the applause.

Brianna was wearing a sky-blue shirt that perfectly matched her eyes, and a pink scarf that made her cheeks look even more flushed than usual. Her hair was smooth and shiny; her speech was perky and filled with spirit. Everything about her seemed presidential. She couldn't have been a more perfect candidate. Which made sense, since she had always been perfect at everything she tried.

It was one of the reasons I hated her.

Except that I didn't hate her. Not anymore. Before, I might have thought that her speech was totally fake, just like her. But I knew now that Brianna actually believed the stuff she was saying. She believed in the winter carnival and the spring dance. She believed that the class council really did give students a voice.

Brianna *wanted* to be president, and that's why she was running.

So, I asked myself one last time, *why am I?*

"Thank you, Brianna," Mr. Hamilton said as Brianna finished her speech — and got a standing ovation. Fine with me. The longer they clapped, the longer I had before it was my turn. I tried to distract myself by focusing on Mr. Hamilton. Today's

T-shirt was orange, with the Trix cereal rabbit dancing across the front. Definitely an eight. Maybe even a nine. I guess he felt like he had to dress up for the big assembly, because he'd thrown a brown corduroy jacket over the T-shirt. But at least there was no tie. Mr. Hamilton in a tie would have looked like Fish in a dress — just wrong.

"And now, we'll hear from Callie Singer," Mr. Hamilton announced. He turned toward me and winked. "Ready?" he mouthed.

No.

I nodded.

For a moment, I wanted to jump out of my seat and run away. But instead, I stood up and walked slowly to the podium. Mr. Hamilton gave me a little thumbs-up as I passed him. It would have looked kind of dorky on anyone else, but he just made it seem cool. And it was more than that: He seemed like he meant it. Like he wanted me to do a good job — maybe he even wanted me to win. I was pretty sure teachers weren't supposed to have an opinion on that kind of thing. But people don't always do what they're supposed to do.

I should know.

I gripped the edges of the podium and peered out at the audience. Hundreds of faces stared back at me.

I gulped.

Fish and Max were sitting front row, center. Max saluted. Fish crossed his eyes and stuck out his tongue. I choked back a laugh.

And just like that, I knew what I had to do.

Or make that: what I wanted to do.

I folded up my speech and slipped it into my pocket. Then I took a deep breath. It was time to say what I wanted to say, just like I used to do, before this whole thing started.

It was time to start acting like Callie Singer again.

"You don't want to vote for me," I said into the mike. There was a soft whine of feedback. I winced, but kept going. "Not unless you want a president who thinks the whole *idea* of class council president is kind of lame." I wanted to look out at the audience, to see how people were reacting — but I was afraid that if I stopped talking, I might never start again. So I just stared out into the distance and kept going.

"I didn't even want to run for seventh grade president, not at first. The only reason I did was to beat Brianna. I didn't think about what would happen if I won, or whether I would be a good president. I didn't really care. I just wanted to win. So I did everything I could think of to get your votes. I started dressing different and talking different.

I started acting like someone I thought you wanted me to be. But not anymore. This is who I am."

I stood up straighter. "I'm Callie Singer, and I don't like dances, I don't like carnivals, I don't like extracurricular activities or gym class or cheer-leaders or pep rallies. I don't like people who care too much about being popular, and I think school spirit is annoying. I think our school colors are ugly, and it's totally embarrassing that our football team has never won a game. Or at least, it would be embarrassing if I cared about sports, but I don't.

"So if you want a president like that, if you want a president who doesn't even really know what a president's supposed to do, but probably won't like doing any of it, if you want a president who thinks we'd be better off spending fund-raising money on better cafeteria food or a DVD collection for the library than a stupid dance that no one wants to go to, anyway, then you should vote for me. But otherwise, you should probably vote for Brianna." I was about to leave the stage, but I realized that I hadn't finished yet. If I was going to tell the truth, I had to tell *all* of it.

"Oh, and one more thing," I said. "I'm the one who ruined all of Brianna's posters. I got carried away. It was dumb and it was wrong, and I'm sorry." I swung around to face Brianna, and said it again.

"I'm sorry." She looked like she was struggling to give me the standard Brianna Blake smile, but her face was frozen in a look of shock, with her eyes wide and her mouth curled into a perfect *O*. I liked her better that way — at least it was real.

I turned back to the audience. "What it comes down to is that you should vote for whoever you want. I know I will."

The auditorium was dead silent.

Principal McCourt glared at me, and I had a feeling that there was another meeting in the principal's office in my future. Mr. Hamilton just shook his head, looking kind of disappointed. The audience remained completely still.

Until two people, sitting front row center, stood up. They started to cheer.

After Brianna's speech, the whole room had jumped to its feet, clapping and hollering. All I got were Fish and Max, slapping their hands together over their heads and shouting at the top of their lungs.

I guess it wasn't much of a standing ovation.

But it was enough for me.

We voted in social studies class, right after the morning assembly. Mr. Hamilton handed out the ballots at the end of the period.

"Good luck to both our candidates," he said as he walked up and down the aisles, laying the slips of paper on our desks. When he got to my desk, he paused and spoke in a voice so quiet that only I could hear. "That was quite a speech."

I didn't want to look at him. "I messed up," I mumbled. "Not with the speech. Before, with the campaign. I just thought if I said the right thing this morning, maybe I could fix it."

"Well . . . it's a start." Mr. Hamilton handed me my ballot. "A good one." I finally looked up. He was smiling. "Good luck, Callie."

"I'm going to need more than luck," I said. "Especially now that the whole school's seen the *real* Callie Singer."

"I think the real Callie's got more fans than she thinks," Mr. Hamilton said. "So hopefully, this time, she's planning to stick around for a while."

I ran a hand through my hair, which was spiky and uncombed again, just the way I liked it. "Don't worry, Mr. Hamilton. From now on, she's not going anywhere."

"So, I'm thinking pity party tonight at eight?" I suggested to Max and Fish. We were sitting in our last period study hall, waiting for the election results to be announced. Some study hall teachers make you sit silently doing your homework. But Ms. Lee, our teacher, spent most study hall periods sitting on her desk reading *Celebrity Beat* magazine. She didn't care what we did, as long as we didn't bug her. It wasn't much of an educational philosophy — but it beat homework. "We'll rent bad horror movies with lots of fake blood, Max can cook up her famous burnt popcorn, and I'll supply the ice cream. Lots and lots of ice cream," I added.

"Pity party?" Fish said. "But what if you win?"

I gave him a look. Max shook her head. "I don't think we need to worry about that."

Before Fish could say anything else, Brianna appeared next to our desks. "So you're coming tonight, right?" she asked, looking at Fish.

He looked clueless.

"To my party?" she added.

"Isn't it a little soon to be inviting people to your victory party?" Max said. "You could still lose." I knew she didn't believe it, but she sure sounded like she did.

Brianna's cheeks turned pink. "Oh. Well, it's not officially a victory party. I'm just . . . you know. My dad wanted . . ." She shrugged. "Any excuse to have a party, right?"

Fish scratched the side of his head. "I'd like to, Brianna, but I've kind of got other plans. . . ."

"It's okay," I said. And I was surprised to realize that I meant it. It really *was* okay. "I don't care if you want to go —"

"But you have to come, too!" Brianna chirped.

"What?"

"You and Max," she said. "You're *all* invited."

"You can't invite us to your victory party," Max pointed out. "If you win, that means we lose. That's the opposite of victory. That's defeat."

Brianna shrugged. "Even losers like cake, right?"

Max opened her mouth, but I jumped in first. I knew Brianna hadn't meant to call us losers. At least, I was pretty sure.

"Would you really want me at your party?" I asked. "Even after what I did?"

Brianna nodded. "I'm sure."

"Brianna?" Britney called out from across the room. "Do you want pink streamers or purple?"

"And should the cake have just your face on it or your whole body?" Ashton chimed in.

"If it's your whole body, we have to pick out your outfit?" Britney screeched.

Brianna blushed and looked back at us. "I should probably . . ."

"Yeah," I said. "Well. Good luck, I guess."

"You too," Brianna said. She held out her hand

and I shook it. "May the best candidate win, right?"

"You know what?" For the first time in my life, I gave Brianna Blake a real smile. It wasn't toothpaste-commercial white, or pep-rally wide. But it was 100 percent real and 100 percent me. A Callie Singer original. "I think she will."

"Attention, students." The PA system crackled to life. "The votes have been tallied. We will now announce the winners of the seventh grade class council elections."

Brianna ran across the room to huddle with Britney and Ashton. Max squeezed my shoulder. Fish winked. And me?

I couldn't breathe. I didn't know what I was more afraid of — losing or winning. I just knew I wanted it to be over.

But that wasn't going to happen anytime soon. Instead, the principal droned on and on about the democratic process and civic responsibility. Then, veeeeerrrrrrry slooooooowly, he announced the winners of all the other races. What was he trying to do to me?

I wasn't the only one suffering. Across the room, Brianna had been holding her breath so long she'd practically turned blue. Next to me, Max had clenched her fists so tightly that if she'd had any

166

kind of nails, she would have dug holes in her palms. Even Fish looked nervous — although only a best friend could tell. When he was nervous, he looked pretty much the same as he always looked, except that his left knee jiggled up and down. And as the principal droned on, Fish's knee jiggled like a jackhammer. But was he nervous for me, or for Brianna?

Probably for both of us, I reminded myself. *And that's okay.*

"Both presidential candidates should be congratulated for their strong campaigns," the principal finally said. "The election was decided on a single vote!"

I could hear Britney and Ashton gasp. They'd thought it was going to be a landslide. And who could blame them?

"But every vote counts, and winning by one is still winning. So let's all congratulate the new president of the seventh grade class . . ."

I held my breath.

I closed my eyes.

I squeezed my hands into fists.

"Brianna Blake!"

☆ CHAPTER ELEVEN ☆

Brianna's victory party was exactly what you'd expect. Pink and purple streamers and balloons everywhere. Tea lights floating in a gigantic outdoor pool. Gourmet chocolates and a giant cake with Brianna's face drawn in frosting. Cheerleaders and jocks flirting with one another under weeping willows. And everywhere you looked, giant banners that read CONGRATULATIONS PRESIDENT BLAKE! Totally Brianna.

Totally repulsive.

But I had to admit the cake was good.

And Brianna seemed honestly happy that we showed up. Fish, Max, and I arrived together, and Brianna met us at the door. "I'm so glad you came!" she gushed. She grabbed my hand and pulled me to a quiet corner of the room. "You're not too upset, are you?" she asked. "About the election?"

People had been asking me that all day, and I told them all the same thing. "I'll live."

She whooshed out a sigh. "Good. So I was thinking, your speech this morning? It was kind of . . . um, different. But you have a lot of really strong opinions. I could use that. So I thought maybe I could appoint you to the class council as, like, a special advisor or something?"

"Really? *Me?*" I was flattered — and totally surprised. For a second, I even thought about saying yes. Even though the whole election thing had been kind of a disaster, people did *listen* to me for once. I liked that part of it. But that was the only part.

And that wasn't enough.

"It's not for me," I told her. Politics was Max's thing, just like art was Fish's thing. And my thing? I guess I still didn't have one. But at least I knew what I *didn't* want: I didn't want to do any more lying or any more sucking up or any more pretending to be someone I wasn't. I wanted to be me, whoever that turned out to be.

So that was a start.

Brianna's face fell. She still wasn't used to people saying no. "Really? It's not just the speech. Your campaign was kind of awesome. You were really good at strategizing and all that —"

That's when I had my first and last great idea of the campaign season. "You really want a special advisor who knows what she's talking about?" I asked. I shot a look across the room at Max. "You want someone loud and opinionated who knows something about everything and can always figure out exactly what to do next?"

Brianna nodded eagerly. "That's what I'm saying! So you'll do it?"

"Not me," I said, giving her a mysterious smile. "But I've got the perfect person for the job."

The party at my house later that night was slightly different. Brianna had seventy-five guests; I had two. But they were the only two I needed.

"You *sure* you're not upset?" Max asked me for about the seven hundredth time. We had just finished watching *Zombie Killers from Venus!* and were about to start *Vampire Babies Ate My Brains!* It was the perfect double feature.

"I'm sure," I told her, yet again. "Are you sure *you're* not mad that I messed things up by giving that speech?"

Max laughed. "Please, that speech turned out to

be the best campaign strategy of all! People loved it."

"Yeah, I got that from all the cheering and applause," I joked.

"No, she's right," Fish said. "People were surprised, but once they thought about it, they were really impressed that you had the nerve to stand up and say what you thought. I know I was."

"Me too," Max said. "I just wish I'd thought of it sooner — we might have won. Maybe if I'd been a better campaign manager . . ."

"You were the perfect campaign manager," I assured her.

"Except for that whole diaper thing," Fish added in a stage whisper. I smushed a pillow in his face.

"I don't care that I lost," I said. "The only thing I care about is that everything's back to normal with us. And that we're never going to fight again. Right?"

"Right," Fish agreed.

Max crinkled her forehead. "Well, statistically, that seems kind of unlikely —"

"Max!" Fish and I shouted.

"Never again," Max said, holding up her hand like she was giving a solemn oath. "I swear."

Okay, we all knew it wasn't true. Best friends fight sometimes. It's just as much a part of being friends as watching zombie movies and scarfing popcorn. But I promised myself that no matter how much we fought, we would always make up. Because best friends do that, too.

I flopped back on the couch, with my head on Max's lap and my legs propped on Fish's shoulders. He shoved them away, but I put them back.

"Your feet stink," he complained.

"That's why they like hanging out with you," I joked. "They fit right in."

So he grabbed hold of my ankle and tickled the bottom of my foot until I finally jerked it away. Max isn't the only one who's good at strategy, I guess.

"This is pretty much perfect, isn't it?" I asked, when I stopped giggling and caught my breath again. "Too bad we can't have a pity party every night."

"*Almost* perfect," Max said, shaking her head. "'Perfect' would have been a three-person *victory* party. I still can't believe you only lost by one vote. It's crazy. You gave that speech practically begging people not to vote for you, and almost half the class still did!"

"Yeah," I pointed out. "Almost." I shuddered, thinking how close I'd come to winning. What would I have done *then*?

"Just one vote," Max muttered. "If we'd gotten just *one* more . . ."

"Hey, don't look at me!" Fish protested. Max hadn't asked him who he voted for. But I guess she couldn't help wondering. "I may have been working for Brianna's campaign, but I voted for you, Callie. I swear."

"I know." And I did. I wasn't worried anymore about Brianna stealing him away. Fish was just the kind of guy who liked being friends with everyone. But at the end of the day, I knew he'd always end up here on the couch with me and Max, watching bad movies and eating burnt popcorn. Because just like us, that's where he really wanted to be.

"I wish you had won," Fish said. "I still say Brianna's okay. But you would have made a great president. I mean it."

"Thanks." I hung my head, trying to pretend I was truly sad about my defeat.

But that's the thing about best friends: You can't fool them. Max tipped her head to the side and narrowed her eyes.

"Wait a second," she said. "Who did *you* vote for?"

I couldn't help it — I laughed. "I'll never tell."

And I never did.

☆ ABOUT THE AUTHOR ☆

Robin Wasserman has never received a single vote for anything, from anyone. (Of course, she has also never run for anything, so that might be why.) She does, however, think she would make an excellent president of . . . something. She's just not sure what. While she's figuring that out, she bides her time living in New York, writing series like Chasing Yesterday, and deciding who should get her vote.